SLANTED

Threads That Bind

VERNELL WEST

Westwinn
Portland, OR

ACKNOWLEDGEMENT

I want to thank all those who offered feedback and insights to help me shape this book. They are a few of the golden threads in the tapestry that is my life.

Contents

Chapter 1- Sleight of Hand

Alex Lawson remembered his daughter's warm smile and soft voice. To him, her smile was like a flicker of light that pierced the darkness and her voice like the stillness of the night. Even though she was 25, he was still almost defenseless against Lydia's requests for something (anything) that he did not wish to give her. It had always been this way since she was a little girl. He remembered her tiny voice melting his heart like warm oil massaged over tense muscles. It relaxed him. Her voice and smile were too much for him to resist. He would willingly concede to her requests as kinked muscles yield to the touch of warm oil in skilled hands. He laughed as his mind went back to when she was five, how she convinced him to get her a puppy while they were living in an apartment that did not allow it. Or when she was in college, to make rent payments for one of her friends for three months while her parents went through a messy divorce. It was her friend's last term before graduating and Lydia insisted that they would graduate together. "We're sooo close! Don't quit now," Lydia pleaded. "It's not fair that your dad cut you off just 'cause he's angry at your mom. I'm sure I can convince my dad to help." And so, she did.

His memories were mixed with sadness and pride. Tears slowly rolled down his cheeks at the thought that she was no longer with him. He tried hard to remember every little detail about her since her birth as though this would blunt the sharp impact of her death. His mind went back to when she was born, her first steps, her first words, her favorite foods, her graduation from high school, from college and how happy she was to be a graphic artist and volunteer tutor. She was a beautiful person with an engaging personality that attracted many, especially young men. She was a petite brunette, five-feet two inches tall, curvaceous, and well-endowed. She usually dressed casually, jeans, sneakers and loose-fitting t-shirts or sweatshirts. For business occasions, she would wear professional pant suits with just the right tailoring to de-emphasize her breasts.

Lydia loved her father and appreciated all that he did for her. She could not remember her mother who died in an automobile accident a few months after her birth. Lydia knew her name only (Olivia) and the circumstances of her death. Olivia was instantly killed in a collision when the driver of a small truck blew through a stop sign as mother and baby were on their way to a scheduled doctor visit. The baby was seated in the rear and was unharmed. At home, there were pictures of her in old photo albums that her dad kept on a book shelf in the living room. From time to time Lydia would look through them to see Olivia with her dad in wedding pictures or alone smiling or dancing. Her mother loved to dance. She would also ask her dad questions about pictures of Olivia with other family members in Spain. He would identify each person by name, her parents, brothers and sisters.

Lawson, now looking through the albums suddenly realized that his wife and daughter both died at age 25. Lydia was nearly a spitting image of her mother at that age. There was just a slight difference in their physical characteristics. Olivia was much darker and had dimples when she smiled.

In college, Lydia studied philosophy, psychology and graphic arts. Four years later she received a bachelor in philosophy and graphic arts and minor in psychology. Her chosen fields of study were so exciting to her that the four years were a blur. There was so much more that she wanted to learn. She decided to continue learning in a work environment where she could satisfy her curiosity and use her creative skills as a graphic artist. She got a job at Feltonia Community College as a graphic artist and volunteered as a tutor for students working towards their GED. Once when asked by her father what her plans were she responded: "I am going to get a master's degree in psychology but meanwhile I am going to learn all I can about what motivates people to do what they do, how they think, and how they express themselves in the real world. I think working with young people that have some issues but are trying to better themselves in a GED program can give me an unfiltered view of this. Of course, my graphic arts job pays the bills and gives me a creative outlet. I am just getting paid to have fun while trying to make a positive difference."

During her college years, she visited her relatives one summer in Ronda, Spain. Lydia had learned to speak Spanish in high school and from her summer visits to Mexico with her father since she was twelve years old. Olivia's parents, uncles and aunts were overjoyed to meet Lydia and insisted that she extend her two-week visit to ten weeks. Meeting Lydia for the first time, her grandmother cried and hugged her tightly. Lydia reminded her of her Livie, the name her daughter had been known by since she was an infant. She also met older and younger cousins who were eager to show her around the city, exposing her to Spanish culture, cuisine, and architecture. She noticed that most of her relatives were dark-skinned with varying degrees of curly black hair. Her grandparents were first generation Spaniards from Morocco. They spoke both Spanish and Arabic. Lydia was distinguished easily by her lighter skin and full bosom. Her appearance was popular among the local males. This was initially flattering but would later be bothersome to her. She learned from her female cousins how to minimize attention from the opposite sex by dressing in loose fitting attire. She also learned that regardless of her dress that if she wanted to avoid unwanted attention she could do so with the escort of a male cousin. While in Spain she willingly sampled foods foreign to her and learned to actively listen to the views of others which were often radically different than or surprisingly identical to her own. Her visit to Spain was a stark contrast to her life in the states.

4

Now, sitting in court listening to the prosecutor bring charges against a young man for raping, killing and robbing his daughter, Lawson looked at the accused. The last name of the accused sounded familiar. He looked at the people sitting directly behind him and grew faint. They were among some of his first victims. Many years had passed, but he began to remember a family with a little boy and girl who needed money for repairing a furnace in the heart of winter. The mother was a maid and the father a construction worker. A friend who employed the mother told him at a party that she felt sorry for the family, and wished that she could help the family get a new furnace. He told her that he would see what he could do.

He remembered the little boy as quiet and well-mannered. He also remembered him following his father as he showed Lawson the old furnace which no longer worked. It was the middle of winter and the house was drafty, much colder than outside in the sun on the wintry day. The boy was with him when he signed the contract for financing the furnace. The father's signature was barely legible as he shivered in the drafty old house. He had not read the contract, but relied on Lawson's statement that he would be able to easily pay it back in two years.

Lawson had gotten rich through his deception, destruction, and the death of others. He had driven some to excessive drinking and divorce, and others to socially unacceptable and criminal behavior ending in imprisonment or death. The subsequent circumstances of his unsuspecting victims were unknown to him, and he did not care to know of their plight. Whether by taking their properties, or through financial enslavement of others, he was proud of his accomplishments. Lawson contracted with people using difficult to understand clauses and terms that could not reasonably be met. His approach was to find people in desperate financial need with very little understanding of contracts and business, people who were simple laborers and could not afford an attorney to review any agreement. He would ensnare them by providing the money that they needed, all the while knowing that the interest clauses would prevent timely payment in full, and would allow him to take their property, or make it virtually impossible to satisfy the debt over a reasonable period of time.

Lawson breathed a sigh of relief when the contract was signed. He knew that the mother, who barely made minimum wages, and the father who worked seasonally in construction, would not be able to pay the money back. He made sure of this by inserting a clause that would inflate the interest rate should a single payment be missed or late during the contract period. The convenient result would be that this unsophisticated client would then owe him the remaining principle plus a bloated and unanticipated interest payment in the last month of the contract. "Candy from a baby," he thought with a smug, self-satisfaction. He smiled as he thought about the location of the house because he knew that the City had immediate plans to gentrify the neighborhood.

For many years, the City allowed the public infrastructure to deteriorate so much so that the banks were unwilling to invest in needed improvements to personal property. Street surfacing, signs and lighting remained in need of repair and maintenance. The neighborhood was reported on nightly in the local news. The news coverage seemed comprised mostly of intermittent shootings and prostitution. It did not matter that the shootings were rare and limited to just a few blocks. Although the neighborhood was reputed by the news as undesirable, police officers knew the real story. They preferred to respond to a call to this neglected neighborhood rather than the one to the south, because they were not likely to be met with guns in response to their arrival on the scene. This was so despite negative news coverage that gave the neighborhood a bad reputation among those who did not live there or regularly visit. It did not matter that prostitution thrived openly and was a service provided almost exclusively to men residing from more affluent neighborhoods who created and sustained demand for it. They seduced young, impoverished and uneducated women with their money. Public health and safety was meager for so long that property values declined drastically. People with meager financial means, exploitative slumlords and some who were not readily accepted by the cultural mainstream were attracted to the neighborhood. Because of the continued deterioration of the neighborhood, it was difficult, if not impossible, for residents to purchase property insurance and security services. These services were priced so high that most could not afford them. He knew that it would soon be the hottest real estate market in the city, if not the state. He planned to (and in fact did) on the twenty-fourth month, take ownership of the property. He remembered how proud he was in taking ownership and in anticipating how he would negotiate the re-sale of the property. He was in a strong negotiating position. He had acquired many properties in the neighborhood this way. He once financed a widow who needed a roof repaired, and after two years took possession of her property. Although he did not know it, the widow, Sasha Winston, died not long after moving in with relatives.

Looking at the accused, his mind went back to the little boy who was shivering as he held the hand of his father. Not even the shivering could hold back the warmth of his smile as he watched his father sign the contract. He could hear the child who was only five years old say to his grandmother who lived with her son and his wife, "Granny, we gonna get warm now." He turned loose his father's hand and went to give his grandmother a big hug. She kissed his cold face as he said, "Daddy's gonna make your cold nose warm again." She laughed and said, "Sho'nuf." She looked forward to the warmth. Over the last month, her only warmth had come at night when she would snuggle under bundles of blankets. During the day, she did household chores and took care of the little boy while his sister was at school, the mother at work, and the father looking for work. His thoughts came to a screeching halt as he listened to the prosecutor.

"Lydia was a young lady who spent much of her free time helping the less fortunate despite the objections of her father. She wanted to make a difference. She wanted to motivate and inspire young people to be the best that they could be. She tutored and mentored young and aspiring college students like the accused, to show them that through hard work, diligence, and perseverance they too could attain wealth and success one day. She pointed to her father as a good role model; somebody who started off with nothing, but by helping others, he successfully built a financial empire."

He was no longer listening to the prosecutor, but was questioning his own integrity, and pondering how his little girl breathed her last breath. *Did she breathe it in fear? Did she call out for me? Did she know that I was not who she thought I was? How did she find out? Did she know that my success came at the expense of others? Maybe she did not know. Did she die because she did not know? Know that I am a phony? That I prey on the helpless? That my victims are my pipeline to success and riches?* Had his deceit and exploitation cost him the ultimate prize, his Lydia? She had been his pride and joy. Yes, it was true that when he first started he had nothing. He had scraped money together to complete college and learned that financial leveraging was a quick path to riches. Ethics were not anything he considered as long as there was no crime. He had schooled his daughter in financial leveraging, but left out any reference to unethical inflated interest rates and impossible cumulative balloon payments. He never mentioned that the scales were unbalanced against the unsuspecting. He would appear as a sheep, but the wolf in him would terrorize his vulnerable prey who were helpless to respond. Because he withheld this information, his daughter naively thought she could help the less fortunate using him as an icon. He felt overcome with guilt, not knowing if he had set in motion the acts that led to her death. At that moment, he was overwhelmed with regret. Had a life-time of smoke and mirrors taken what he most cherished? Prosperity and status could not fill the hole her absence left. Sadness and anger contended with his guilt over her loss. His soul was adrift, searching for something to hold on to.

His memory flashed back to the names of the family members; James Waters and wife Ora Waters. They lived with their two children and James' mother, Oletha Waters, a widow. Their daughter's name was Linda and Justin was the boy's name--Justin, who was now accused of these ugly crimes against Lydia Lawson. Lawson now clearly remembered the family in detail.

10

He could hear Waters say, "Justie, Mr. Lawson is gonna help us make the house warm again." Justin and his sister started a sing-song chant "warm all over, warm in the morning, warm at night, warm all over, gonna be warm again."

Chapter 2 - Soil and Roots

Sasha Winston, forced to move in with relatives, had never lived alone. Her seven-year-old grandson, Cleotus, lived with her. She had raised the boy since he was three. The boy had only a faint memory of his mother who was lost to a drug over-dose just after his third birthday. Her name was Bella Winston. She had been impregnated with Cleotus by a local young man who moved away shortly before the birth of the child. He was urged to leave by his mother for personal safety. He and the child's mother (who was only fifteen at the time) were from two feuding families, the Masters and the Winstons. The Masters denied that the child was a Masters and said that the mother was a "drug-head who opened her legs for anybody." The Winstons alleged that the mother was raped, and could not deny the child's resemblance to Jake Masters, especially as the he grew older. Bella had ignored the feud, named the child Cleotus Masters, and listed Jake Masters as the father on the birth certificate. She was raised to tell the truth, no matter the circumstances. To name her son Cleotus Winston would be an obvious lie that could not be justified, ever. She was a beautiful young girl who had grown up alone with her mother. Her father had died of an aneurysm before her birth.

Cleotus was called Cleo, and by age eighteen had still never seen his father. He only knew that his grandmother had often said,

"You look just like your daddy, Jake." Since the death of his grandmother, he was raised in two different foster homes. His initial placement was in a family that had two children, a boy and girl who were two to three years older than him. The placement lasted only three months and abruptly ended when the parents found out he was a descendant of two feuding families across town. He spent the next year in a home for orphaned children. He was again taken in and later adopted by a family with a girl and boy. He was only a couple of years older than them. The young parents were fully aware of his background and circumstances under which he was placed in foster care. As though he were their biological child, they loved and cared for him. The nine-year-old was made to feel welcome by their two biological children, and in a short while, they began treating him like an older brother. Over the years, the parents researched his short history of the time he lived with his grandmother. They helped him understand where he came from all the while making clear that should he want to learn more about his biological family he could do so when he was eighteen, and they would help. They changed his name to "Cleo Waters."

Jake Masters learned of the boy's adoption years later. He set out to find where he was placed. He found out that Cleo was placed with a family living in his old neighborhood. Cleo was almost eighteen at the time. Jake contacted the family to arrange to meet Cleo. The adopted father, James Waters, answered the phone, "Mr. Masters, I do not have any objection to your meeting Cleo--after he turns eighteen--if that is what he wants. We have shared with him who his biological father is over the years. If he meets with you after he is eighteen that will be his decision. As you know, he will be eighteen in August."

James told Cleo of Jake's request. He reminded him that whatever decision he made, James and his wife would support him. A couple of weeks later, Cleo told his father that he would like to meet with Jake in the presence of his father and mother. James replied that he thought it was a wise and mature decision. He then gave Cleo the number to contact Jake and make arrangements for the meeting. Cleo and Jake agreed to meet months later at James' home. It would be two weeks after his eighteenth birthday, Jake knocked on the front door of the Waters' residence. The entire family was eagerly anticipating his visit. Justin and Linda were excited to meet Jake, though their parents were cautiously reserved. They were all amazed at the uncanny resemblance of Jake and Cleo. It was as though they were seeing Cleo in a mirror some twenty years into the future. He lacked only Jake's mustache and beard. Jake noted that the mannerisms of Cleo, Justin and James were identical. The two boys were distinguished only by their physical appearance; Justin was five feet six inches and Cleo six feet five inches. Jake was careful not to show any resentment that he harbored towards James, but he was irritated observing Cleo's mannerisms imitating those of James.

In the coming months, Cleo would meet with Jake once monthly outside of the home, usually at a restaurant or park. He asked Jake many questions concerning his family history and what his mother was like. Jake filled in some of the many gaps in Cleo's knowledge of his family history. He learned that his natural ability to debate came from the Masters, and his love for and ability to do art was from his mother's side of the family, the Winstons. It quietly irked Jake that during the many months meeting with Cleo that Cleo never once called him father. He always referred to James as "Dad" or to his siblings as "Lil' brother" and "Sis."

Chapter 3 - Infertile Ground

She tasted something wet, warm, and salty flowing down her cheeks, over her chin and down her throat; her dry lips, now moistened with a flood of water from her eyes, quivered as she gathered herself, quickly put on her clothing and left. Jake remembered lying still, as if he were asleep, listening to her whimper, and opening his eyes at the sound of the door closing. He never saw her again.

Taking a drag of a cigarette that he lit as Cleo asked him why the Winstons and Masters did not like each other, Jake inhaled deeply and delayed responding. He did not know exactly, but when he was a boy he heard that a Winston had walked in on a Masters in bed with his wife and killed both of them. He was sentenced to life in prison. The dead man had many brothers who were not satisfied with the life-sentence of the Winston and sought revenge. The Masters brothers raped the man's sister, strung her out on drugs, and one of them became her pimp. "She was killed turning a trick a year or so before you were born." He said that the man's mother, a widow, moved to town and vowed to avenge her daughter's death. He took another big puff of the cigarette, flicked it away; slowly pushing the smoke into his nasal passages and lungs, and relaxing with his eyes closed, he blew it out, little by little. He quickly opened his eyes, looked directly at Cleo and calmly told him that the feud was why he could not stay

16

around for his birth. "Things were not too good. My mother begged me to leave town." He avoided telling him that Bella Winston had not been interested in him, that she had resisted his crude juvenile advances each day as she walked home from school. She would not even look at him as he spoke. One day he and she were at a house party when he asked her to dance. She danced with him once, and was careful not to touch him. The house was filled with many people that she knew (Winstons, Masters and others). After the dance she accepted a drink from Jake. The next morning, she woke up naked and in bed with him, her clothing strewn about the room.

Nine months later Bella delivered a baby boy, two months before her sixteenth birthday. She dropped out of school to take care of the baby. Since that night with Jake her high grades had started dipping to "pass" or "unsatisfactory" only. Before, she had received only the highest marks and was recognized as the brightest student in her class. She had loved learning but lost all interest in school as she experienced changes in her body with the pregnancy. Her interest faded as the pregnancy progressed until finally it vanished. She blamed herself for the pregnancy, for allowing herself to be victimized by Jake. She was most troubled with having no memory of the night spent in the room with Jake. She remembered waking up late the following morning (about eleven-thirty) disoriented, and upon discovering where she was and with whom, her eyes welled up.

Leaving the room, she was not familiar with the surroundings. She found out that she was in a neighborhood about ten miles from her home. She had no memory of leaving the party, only of dancing with Jake and accepting a drink from him. Her thoughts haunted her. *How could I be with him? That monster! I would never give him the time of day. Oh! That drink!* She then knew why she could not remember. *He put something in it!*

Sasha watched Bella closely as she observed her daughter who was no longer a top-notch student, spontaneous, lively and engaging. She was now withdrawn, introspective and unmotivated. As she nursed her baby she could barely look at him (for no more than a minute or two at a time). She would think of being with Jake but dreaded imagining what it must have been like. This brought hot tears to her eyes and blinding anger as her mind played back the details of the party, the nothingness of the night in the room with Jake, and the heart-break of the following morning.

One afternoon while Sasha was watering her small vegetable garden Bella ran water in the bath tub and got in fully clothed as it was running. The water ran over the top of the tub and flooded the bathroom and hallway floors. Sasha found Bella in the tub staring into space and crying. She took her to the doctor and he diagnosed her with suffering from acute anxiety. He also told Sasha that Bella exhibited symptoms of post-traumatic stress.

18

When Cleo was two years old Bella was hospitalized for a nervous breakdown. Sasha found her at the kitchen table staring into space with tears running down her face. "Bella, baby, you alright?" She did not respond to her mother's call. She just stared straight ahead without batting an eye. "Bella, what's wrong?" But she knew. The depression and sadness had enveloped her daughter since the night with Jake. Her condition grew worse with time. Sasha had taken her to the doctor a year earlier for depression. She was given anti-depression medication, and Sasha was advised to watch her closely. Months later Bella stopped taking the medicine because it made her gain weight, sapped her energy, and dulled her senses. She was careful not to let her mother know. Six weeks without the medicine cleared her mind and allowed it to constantly play back the events that led to her pregnancy. Finally, they replayed over and over again like a scratched record. And like a scratched record needs the needle lifted from the rut, the replay in her mind needed to be stopped. Bella's seven day stay in the psychiatric ward did just that. She was given strong doses of her medication and participated in group therapy. She was then released with instructions to remain on the medication. At home, she remained on her medication for about two months. During the first week of the relapse her mind was clear. She knew that the only way to remain stable was to take her medicine, but she also knew that she would not be fully aware and in

19

control of her mind. Yet she knew that not taking the medicine would let her mind slip away from her. She calmly decided to write a letter to her mother.

Mommy, I know that you love me, and I love you more than anything. I also love Cleo, but every time I look at him it's like falling off of a cliff. My beautiful baby boy, my beautiful baby boy ... He needs more than I can give him. I'm sorry for making your life so sad. I don't seem to fit in anywhere any more. Tell Cleo when he is older that I am sorry. I love him, but it's just not enough. And Mommy, don't be sad. This is best for both of us, and Cleo. Your loving baby girl, Bella.

She folded the paper and wrote "Mommy" on the back side and placed it face up on the kitchen table. She filled a glass with water, went to her bedroom and swallowed ten pills as she drank the glass of water. She lay on the bed, closed her eyes, relaxed and fell asleep.

Sasha moved in with her sister Anna and husband Abraham when she lost her home to Lawson Associates for failure to keep up with the loan payments for the roof repair. Sasha, yearning for her Bella, confided in Anna who was fifteen years older and like a mother figure. She told her of Bella's nightmares, lack of appetite, episodes staring into space, and neglect in caring for herself or the baby. She would have to constantly remind her to bathe, brush her teeth, comb her hair, and attend to personal hygiene. When she was not crying, or transfixed she was napping. She would get up only at her mother's prompting. She had become almost speechless, even with the baby. Her voice could be heard responding only to Sasha's questions. Her responses were soft and meager, often unheard and prompting the question again. *Did you feed the baby?--Yes.-- Did you change him?-- No.--Don't you think he needs changing?--No.--Don't you think you ought to check?--Don't know.--Please check.--OK.--What do you think about the dress I bought you?--Nice.--What do you like about it?--Don't know, just pretty.*

After a short stay in her sister' s home Sasha died of a stroke. Anna later found among her things the letter written to Sasha from Bella.

Chapter 4 - Blue Skies and Storm Clouds

The Waters got their new furnace with the loan from Lawson's company. The furnace was replaced immediately and the house was warm again. Ora continued working as a maid while James looked for work in construction and for whatever was available. They struggled to make payments for the first six months because James could not find steady work. His mother, Oletha, helped them with the next 12 payments from her savings of a small insurance payout for the death of her husband. James and Ora had reluctantly agreed to accept her help after she convinced them that she was doing it for her grandchildren. "If there was any other way to help them have a chance for a better life than us, I would do it. Take this money and invest in their future. This is what your daddy would do if he was here. "

Over the next six months, things were looking good for the Waters. James found a good construction job and was making good wages. They were able to make the payments with ease and even had a little money left over. James' new employer was pleased with his work and had promoted him to project manager. The company was building houses as fast as possible to keep up with the robust demands of the real estate market. Many of the new houses were constructed on small lots near his home. The neighborhood was dotted throughout with new houses and neighbors. There was a new fire station and police headquarters within blocks of his home. James had worked as a construction laborer on both. It looked as though the Waters ' financial worries were soon to be left in the rear-view mirror. James could now buy Justin and Linda, who were in the first and second grades, new clothing for school. James was feeling relief from his financial woes of the last two years. But that sense of relief faded away just as the final payment was due. The construction company had been sued for defective work by two home owners. It filed for bankruptcy and did not pay its employees, but the company representative explained to the workers that they would receive payment in full, after the case was reviewed by the bankruptcy court. He further explained that the bankruptcy filing was a strategy to re-organize the company to establish a more sound financial footing, and estimated that paychecks would likely be issued in thirty to sixty days.

James contacted Lawson to explain the situation. He assured him that he would make the final payment as soon as he received his paycheck. Lawson was elated at his inability to pay but pretended to be very sympathetic to James' situation. "Don't worry about it. I know you are good for it. You can make the payment later." He knew that James was not aware of the inflated interest clause and the balloon payment terms that transferred ownership if the homeowner did not pay timely. He could see that he would own some prime property that was well-kept and would yield a large profit for a minimal investment.

After all it was in the hottest real estate market in the city and it was a seller's market.

Forty-five days after the due date of the final payment, James received a paycheck from the company. He immediately cashed it and had a cashier's check made out to Lawson's company. While he was working, Ora delivered it to Lawson the following day. He thanked her and asked her to give his regards to James. A few days later James received a certified letter notifying him that because the total payment was not made timely, regrettably the property, as per the terms and conditions of the contract, was being transferred to Lawson Associates. It instructed that all persons and personal property were to be removed within thirty days of the notice. The letter did not say that Lawson filed the necessary legal paperwork on the day that the final payment was due (and forty-six days before receiving James' check) to have the property transferred for the failure of the homeowner to make the final payment.

James and Ora went to Lawson's office to plead for their property. James reminded him of their conversation concerning the final payment and that he was told to pay whenever he received his paycheck. Ora told him that when she delivered the payment that he thanked her and never mentioned that any additional payment was due. Lawson again pretended to be very concerned with the turn of events. "You people are good people and by golly you made your payments on time, all except one. If it were up to me I would chalk this up to a misunderstanding. But unfortunately, it is not up to me. I have to go by the terms of the contract. My partners are insisting on it. They don't understand you folk like I do. I tried talking them out of this but they ain't budging. I am so sorry." James interrupted, "What we gonna do? We cannot afford another house in this here neighborhood. We came here when nobody wanted to live over here. Now the houses have skyrocketed in price. Everybody's tryin' to get in here now. All these young professionals goin' up and down the street, walkin' dogs, pushin' babies and joggin'. Where are we gonna be?" Lawson blurted out, "I am so sorry!" Realizing that he had abruptly interrupted James, he lowered his voice and continued slowly, "There are some more affordable apartments on the South side. Maybe you people can find something over there." The South side was a part of town that was mostly populated by people with low income and where many had relocated as their previous neighborhood became unaffordable because of the increased rents that came with improvements to infrastructure and its appeal to new residents with higher incomes. The Waters' home was in a neighborhood where many of the longtime residents could no longer afford to stay because of gentrification.

James and Ora returned home to tell Oletha the bad news. Oletha had remained hopeful that the Waters could stay in their home of the past decade. Her husband had died a year before she moved in.

The grandchildren represented hope that things would be different in the coming years for her family. Her husband died of a heart-attack, but she believed it was of a broken heart. He had worked multiple jobs to take care of his family, but no matter how hard he worked he struggled to make ends meet. Her countenance changed upon hearing the news. Suddenly, she felt very sad and angry. Her face felt inflamed as though the blood was being drained from it. Nauseated and weak, she braced herself against the kitchen table to steady herself as she slid into a chair to hold her limp body. She slumped over and began to cry softly. Her feeble voice squeaked, "Mercy Lord, mercy Lord, mercy Lord. "

The Waters were bewildered and confused about Lawson's assertion that their home no longer belonged to them. A few days after meeting with Lawson they received a letter from Lawson Associates signed by Lawson, president and CEO, stating that he had convinced his partners to extend the eviction date an additional one-hundred eighty days. He explained that it was an unfortunate situation and that with great reluctance he was forced to move forward with the eviction, but this was the best that he could do. He said that the time extension would hopefully relieve much of the stress brought on with the move. The fact of the matter was that he knew the City would be breaking ground on some major infrastructural improvements near the Waters property in about sixty days. There would be new retail sites, restaurants, and a national bank where there were empty or abandoned lots; condominiums in place of single housing; newly paved roads, improved street signage and lighting; zoning changes to enhance business and residential cohesiveness; and low interest financing available for businesses and home owners. He learned of this through his membership in the Chamber of Commerce, City Club and by serving on various boards for the City. To delay the eviction would allow him to avoid expenses for upkeep of the property and to demand a significantly higher sale price. Meanwhile the Waters would have to pay him rent during the extension.

James, as a construction project manager, was becoming familiar with the management of a company. He had slowly begun reading documents such as change orders in his new role. He learned that oral statements by the owner or their representatives must be included in the written order to be valid. This would minimize disputes and the company's liability. He was in fact promoted to project manager because his predecessor had omitted information in some change orders that resulted in disputes, and ultimately two claims against the company for defective work. James quickly recognized his error when signing the contract with Lawson. He failed to read it, and trusted Lawson's verbal statements. At that point, he reviewed it with haste. There were many things that he did not understand, but he understood that the intent of the inflated interest rate clause was to take his property. He understood that Lawson's niceties were purposeful and consistent with the contract. He was so angry at first that his whole body shook uncontrollably. Then he felt sick. All his strength seemed to leave him. He was nauseous and light-headed. After gathering himself, he determined that he would have signed the contract anyway, even had he read it and had he known what was in it. He would not allow his family to freeze in the cold of winter. His mother, his wife and his children were his life. He would always be there for them. He reluctantly admitted to himself that he should have read the contract. Had he read it Lawson's deception would not have worked.

The spring brought on the sunny weather, flowers blooming and birds singing. People were once again in the streets, parks and malls engaged in activities that pointed to the future. The parks were a magnet for lots of youthful activities (jogging, tennis, basketball) and for picnics. They were no longer cloistered in their homes as they were in the winter. They spent time in the streets and on the sidewalks going to and from parties, churches, and community meetings. The warmth of their homes during the winter was replaced with affection for being with each other. Friendship and fellowship were now the bond. Malls and other small retail outlets attracted many shoppers. They were in search of items that were opposite of the winter. Spring-time meant the winter thaw was over. Shorts, sandals, sleeveless shirts, and ice cream were in popular demand. This was all in contrast to the Waters'

28

activities as they made moving arrangements that would place them across town, in a low-income neighborhood on the South side. The move pointed to the deceit of the past. It weighed heavily on all of them. Apartment living awaited them in an unfamiliar environment. James would have to commute across town to his old neighborhood for work. His wife would have to find more work as a maid and work longer hours to make up for the additional expense of and time on public transit. And the children did not know what to expect of their new school. They only knew that they would leave their friends behind in the old neighborhood. James' mother, at age 70, had lost hope. She had witnessed the death of her husband from a "broken heart," and now was fearful of the same fate for her son. She tried to muster courage by quietly singing, *"By faith we are. By faith we do. By faith we try. By faith we will make it. By faith we will be."* As she hummed, Oletha's mind went back over her life. It had been a hard life ...

Oletha was remembering the time down south when she and her husband were young and in love. They got married when she was sixteen and he was eighteen. She was born in 1930 and he in 1928. Neither she nor he completed high school. Their parents pulled them out of school to work and help support their families. He was the oldest of seven boys and she, the middle child of nine, three boys and six girls. She completed only the eighth grade, and her husband, the fifth. Whether she had to do household chores or to help take care of younger siblings while her parents worked in the fields, or cleaned houses for a living, school was a temporary reprieve from her stay-at-home duties. She often accompanied her mother to work. She remembered her parents coming home dead-tired, and often angry and disgusted with their jobs. They complained of working so hard for so little money. They believed education was the best route to a better future for their children, but could never figure out how to send them to school and make ends meet.

When she was sixteen, Sam Waters, a neighborhood fellow that she had known all her life, asked her father for her hand in marriage. Sam and Oletha had been sweet on each other for years. On Sundays after church he had taken to visiting her, and from time to time (with her father's permission) he would take her out for ice cream or just a walk to be alone with her. Sam was employed and ready to start a family. He had gotten a job working at the local lumber supply store. Over the years, he learned as much as he could about the different kinds of wood and pricing. Sam's familiarity with the intricacies and characteristics of various woods made him a valuable employee. He was the store's most knowledgeable person on house-building materials. Even though he had only completed fifth grade, he easily did all the necessary calculations in his head concerning quantities, dimensions, and geometric designs. Nevertheless, he watched others be promoted over the years while he remained in the position for which he was initially hired. It was humiliating to see those he trained become his boss. Despite this he continued working. He needed the job to take care of his family and send his boy to school. He wanted James to complete high school. He did not want to pull him out (the way his parents did him) for financial reasons. Sam would make whatever sacrifice that was necessary for James' education. He began taking on light construction jobs part-time. His first clients were his good neighbors who hired him to work as a carpenter on their homes. He would work construction from seven to noon, then go to work at the store from two in the afternoon to nine at night.

After over thirty years of this work routine, Sam was hospitalized. He had been working when he complained of heart-burn. He ignored it and continued working, but at noon-time when he was eating lunch with his co-workers, he grabbed his chest and slumped over. Someone immediately called 911 and an ambulance was there in about three minutes. He was told by the doctor caring for him that it was a heart-attack. He would have to stay at the hospital for a few days for observation and to make sure his medications were right. Oletha quickly made her way to the side of her husband. She had long dreaded this day. When she found out it was a heart-attack, she grew faint. Gathering herself, she made brave and said, "We'll be alright, you strong and with the medicine you'll be as good as new in no time." She did not believe her words. Her heart told her differently. Everything would change. He would not be able to do the things most important to him: to work and take care of his family.

She saw a flash of brilliance, sophistication and temperance wrapped in his fervor to care for his family. He demonstrated that he was aware of the present circumstances in which he found himself. Being questioned by a health care professional, he at once gave him the answer he sought while directing the question back to him sprinkled with his life experiences and philosophy. He was now questioning his interviewer who was seemingly helpless to re-gain his position as the interviewer. Questions directed to Sam were answered satisfactorily but prompted him to ask slightly different rhetorical questions of the interviewer. His display of mental clarity and intellectual precision were undeniably on display for all to see and marvel. No one had ever witnessed of him such articulated wisdom. Because Sam refused to agree to work only twenty hours per week when the doctor said it was okay to resume work in approximately six to eight weeks, Oletha was devastated. The brilliance of the moment was bitter-sweet, mournful, and celebratory. The doctor's interview of Sam only confirmed that he was clearly lucid, coherent, and just plain stubborn. His time in the Intensive Care Unit, his failure to be convinced by Oletha and the doctor that less work was for his own good, and his display of mental clarity meant that he was capable of making decisions for himself. He could not be compelled by any medical restrictions to avoid further injury (or death), or convinced even by his wife to comply with the doctor's instructions for his care.

Oletha began thinking about her best friend Emma. Her thoughts of her friend gave her strength as her mind went back to her son and daughter-in-law's insistence that she move in with them after her husband passed away. Life had been good with them and the grandchildren. But Emma, her good friend had not fared so well. She was in her late nineties and a widow for over forty years when her adult children took her properties and home--one of whom took up residence there--and placed her in an assisted living facility.

Emma Masters, at 97 was living with her youngest daughter, Sara Rhines and husband, Andy Rhines. She could no longer live alone. She had been hospitalized and upon being released was carried to her daughter's home, about 60 miles away from her home of over 40 years. Emma's husband had died more than 30 years earlier. She lived alone for almost 25 years without needing or wanting assistance from family. Before staying with her youngest daughter, she had allowed her oldest daughter, Velma Wright, to live with her for more than a year to help her take care of herself. Velma would relocate from another state and spend over a year with her mother cleaning, cooking, making sure she took her medicine and helping her daily with tasks such as bathing and other common, household and personal functions.

Velma, 76, despite being under the doctor's care for high blood pressure and elevated cholesterol had moved over 1,200 miles to care for her mother. She tended to Emma's every need. Ignoring her own health concerns, her sacrifice took its toll. She returned home for respite and to visit her doctor. Less than three months later she suffered a stroke from which she slowly recovered.

A few months after Velma's departure, Sara moved Emma from her home to live with her and husband Andy. Emma did not like being there, and after nearly three years, she asked two of her adult children (Robert and Nadine) to move her out. She had many complaints about her stay at Sara's, and not the least of which was that Sara had prohibited other siblings from visiting her in Sara's home.

Robert Masters and Nadine Raza moved Emma into Robert's home. In tending to their mother's affairs, they discovered that Sara had taken all of Emma's properties and cash. All that remained was two monthly social security checks. Robert and Nadine sought help in sorting through Emma's affairs. They enlisted the help of another sibling, Jake, who though he had left the area years before, joined them and began researching titles to family properties and learned that Sara had taken possession of all of them. In short order, the siblings determined that they needed more help. Jake and Robert appealed to nephew Victor Wright, son of Velma. Despite his mother's

34

disapproving pleas, Victor agreed to help. As money was needed to mount a legal challenge to Sara's title to the family properties, all agreed that anyone who contributed money to re-gain the properties would be reimbursed from the sale of the properties as necessary. This was further commemorated in a Declaration of Property Retrieval signed by Emma that only those contributing would have an equal share in title to the properties after the reimbursement of expenses. It was understood that reimbursement was contingent upon re-possession. Five siblings and Victor (and his wife) contributed.

After almost three years, two law firms, several thousands of dollars in payment of delinquent taxes and legal fees, Victor was able to cause Sara to relinquish the properties. They were given back to the Masters in a limited liability company over which Jake and Nadine controlled. Shortly after the properties were returned, Victor asked his uncle Jake to sell some of the properties to reimburse him and others for the thousands of dollars spent on legal fees, taxes, and related expenses in causing them to be returned to the Masters. Jake chose instead to move into the most valuable property. Nadine, who had contributed a couple of thousand dollars, and at great sacrifice, had relocated from another state to care for her mother, was disappointed with Jake's decision. As a manager in the Masters Limited Liability Company which held title to the properties, and according to the Articles of Agreement, Nadine was authorized to act independently of any other manager. She deeded the properties in the company to Victor. The plan was to sell them and recoup all contributions made to re-possess them from Sara in order to reimburse each contributor. An attempt to sell the most valuable property to ensure enough funds to cover reimbursement expenses was halted by Jake's refusal to allow any realtor to show the property.

Jake moved into the home of his aging mother who had been placed in an assistive living facility. He drank heavily, smoked constantly, and paid no rent. Living off severance pay, and with only utility expenses, he spent his days in conversation with others who did not work but drank their days away. He fancied himself a scholar and superior to his drinking partners. He was often an instigator to the point of angering others. Just at the point where anger leads to brawling, he would diffuse the situation by changing the subject. He had not always done so. When he was younger he once did time in prison for killing a man after a similar instance where he chose to continue instigating. He had grown older and was afraid of going back to prison. He was no longer confident in his ability to fight without looking for some unfair advantage.

When Jake was not instigating or drunk, he began making lots of inquiries of the history of Cleo's family. He eventually learned that the same company that took the boy's maternal grandmother's house had also taken the Waters'.

Chapter 5 - Thinning the Forest

Thinking of her friend' s situation, Oletha gained courage and inspiration. She thought how fortunate she was to be in a family that loved her more than money or things. She had not been left to make it on her own when Sam died, and she had not been invited into her son's home to be exploited. Emma's living arrangement helped her see clearly how blessed she was. James and Ora had asked nothing of her and found it difficult accepting things from her. They wanted only that she be comfortable and safe. Since Sam's death, James, Ora, and the grandchildren had given her love only. She was no longer afraid of what might happen if they had to move from their home. She decided that home indeed was where love lived. Her family was where she found love. She was confident that they would find their way no matter where they lived. She believed in her son as she had believed in her late husband. She knew that he would do whatever was necessary to take care of his family.

Ora knew how much James loved his mother. So, when Oletha's husband died, Ora insisted that James convince her to move in. James did not need any prodding, only to know that he and Ora wanted the same thing. They did what was necessary to overcome the obstacles of everyday living. Some obstacles were to be expected, and they planned for them together. Employment, raising children, and caring for aging parents were all matters to be expected. Although having to move out was unexpected, their remedy was to make the necessary adjustments. In doing so, James assessed why they were being thrown out of their house, and resolved that such a thing would never happen to them again. He would never be gullible and trust the word of another person without knowing the facts and getting some corroborating documentation. He accepted that Lawson had fleeced them out of home and comfort, and the many years of sacrifice and labor by him and his wife seemed lost. He decided that he would take every opportunity offered through his job as project manager to learn about business, contracts, and property acquisition and retention. He vowed that he would never again be duped by the likes of Lawson.

James and his family prepared to move as they went about their normal routine. The children went to school; mom and dad to work, and grandma stayed at home doing her daily chores and organizing for the move. The children were saddened at the thought of leaving their schoolmates behind. They were not their usual happy selves. At recess, they did not join the other children at play. They chose instead to sit on the swing set and slowly swing back and forth, as if swinging would keep things as they were.

At work, James had started taking classes that the company offered. Some of them were at headquarters and others at the local community college. He enrolled in one that his boss was conducting on contract disputes and change orders. Bernie Johnson, his boss, had given up a law career in contract litigation to join the company a few years earlier. He had successfully defended many clients (large companies) that unfairly took advantage of unsuspecting individuals. He had made lots of money, but one day decided that he could no longer stomach it. He had begun seeing in the faces of the defenseless victims, the faces of his family members and friends. No longer a practicing attorney, he chose to use his legal experience to help build communities. He was now a construction manager responsible for managing project managers. During the class he asked James why it was important to get change orders in writing before doing the work. James replied that any work made in reliance on verbal instructions alone that are contrary to the contract would not stand up in court if the work was in dispute. A written agreement is necessary to avoid problems later. Bernie sensed an unusual passion in James' voice and made a mental note to talk with him later. At the end of class, as James was gathering his notes, Bernie approached him and asked had he any experience with change order work that was not under agreement. James told him no, but shared with him the circumstances of the eviction from his home. He told him that he did not review the agreement, but instead relied on Lawson's word, not once but twice. "Now me and my family have to find another place to live." Bernie asked, "Do you mind if I take a look at the agreement?" James told him that he would bring it in the following day. A couple of days later James retrieved a message from his inbox asking him to come to Bernie's office at the end of his work-shift. At the end of his shift, he immediately went to the office.

"James come in, have a seat. I have looked over your agreement with Lawson Associates. As you know by now, this agreement was written to take your property. It could be argued that the terms and conditions are unconscionable as a matter of law--and therefore cannot reasonably be enforced--and that they are particularly unconscionable given Lawson's deliberate misrepresentations. His statement to you that it was alright to make your final payment on a date different than the one stated in the agreement is a substantial alteration of the agreement. Albeit verbal, his acceptance of it would tend to affirm the statement. On the other hand, you could argue that Lawson's statement was fraudulent. In essence, consistent with your 23 previous timely payments, but for his false and deliberately misleading statement you would have made the payment per the agreement. As to taking on Lawson Associates for an unlawful unconscionable contract, misrepresentation, and fraud, it would be very costly, and would take many years to get a ruling, and there's no guarantee that you would win. I think your chances, however, are very good. The good thing about that is that you would be able to stay in your home until there is a ruling. My personal opinion is that you have a winnable case, but I would hate to see you tied up in litigation for years. Litigation can be very strenuous and demoralizing, given the nastiness of the adversarial process. If you decide that this is something you and your wife are prepared to do, I can recommend a good attorney. You can talk it over with your wife and let me know."

"Another alternative is to not fight the eviction. Instead you could use your resources to move ahead. I have spoken with Garrett Hazelton, the company owner, about your predicament. He has offered to sell you a comparable new house that we just completed about ten blocks from your home. He is willing to sell it to you under contract, with monthly payments equal to what you are currently paying. The company would finance the agreement. The total amount that you would pay is 20% more than the cost of building the house. Mr. Hazelton tells me that he knew your father, and because of your father's advice and expertise, his company was launched successfully. He says that he's been watching you and how you manage your projects. They are always completed on time and within budget. Bottom line, he's very impressed with you, as he was with your dad. He wants you to be an integral part of this company."

James sat motionless and unable to speak. He had entered his boss' office with a burden that weighed heavily on him. His world had been turned upside down with the impending move. He had not been able to express the toll of the burden that he was carrying. He

41

knew that his naivete had put his family's welfare in jeopardy, and he could not share it with his wife or mother. He was too ashamed to tell them that he failed to read the agreement. He just put on a brave face to deal with the fallout. The passion detected in his voice while answering a question in the classroom had prompted his boss' interest. A lone tear ran down his cheek as he thanked Bernie, shook his hand, and told him that he would discuss it with his wife. Although he knew which option he was going to choose, he would not share it until after talking it over with her.

Chapter 6 - Arid Earth and Flooding Rain

Now, a dozen years later, Justin was eighteen and in his final month of high school. He was preparing to go to college in the fall. He had achieved high grades and had successfully completed his college entry exams with flying colors. He was accepted in all three universities to which he applied. He knew what kind of career he wanted. Watching his father over the years, and having learned from his grandmother's stories of the struggles and accomplishments of his grandfather, he wanted to be a business owner. He did not remember much about his grandfather, just that he was big. He could also remember seeing his smile and hearing him laugh. His grandfather seldom smiled or laughed, but while playing with his grandchildren he did. His size, smile and hearty laughter made the grandchildren feel safe and happy. Justin did not know exactly what kind of business he would pursue, but the idea of construction ownership appealed to him. He thought of doing his undergraduate studies in architecture or engineering and graduate studies in business or law. He was determined to make his parents proud by earning college degrees through graduate studies. He remembered when he was a child, hearing his grandmother tell him stories of her childhood, how she and his grandfather were unable to attend school regularly. She told him that times were hard, and with no education a person could not expect to make a decent living. Their parents needed the children to work rather than go to school. It was difficult finding a place to rent, pay the bills, and to feed and clothe the family. Children needed to help the family meet financial obligations. She said, "Our parents always wanted an education for us, but could not afford it. At the end of a long and exhausting day, they were too dog-tired to even give it any serious thought."

During the last month of his senior year upon arriving home from school, Justin observed police cars near his home, and as he entered the front door, officers pulled their revolvers and instructed him to raise his hands. Bewildered and frightened, he quickly raised his hands high. At that moment, he saw his grandmother restrained behind a couple of officers, and heard her cry out, "No, no, no, please no, not him." He was handcuffed, read his rights, and told that he was being arrested for the murder, rape, and robbery of Lydia Lawson. He said that he did not know anyone by that name. His grandmother, who had let the officers in, told Justin not to speak. She knew he did not do it. "Your dad will know how to fix this mess."

As her grandson was taken away shackled in a patrol car, Oletha called her son at work. She was unusually calm as she told him of the arrest. Concerned about the stress on his heart, she told him that Justin needed him to be strong, that they would get through it together. "I know he did not do this. You know he did not do this. We must do whatever is necessary to prove it."

James hung up the phone and called Bernie to inform him that he was leaving work early to attend to a family crisis. Bernie, who was now a friend, asked James what was the matter and if he could do anything to help. James told him of the arrest and that he needed to be with his son. While James made his way to the police station, Bernie contacted the company owner. The owner immediately instructed him to call the best criminal defense lawyer that he knew in the state. He made several phone calls.

At the station, James learned that his son was arrested for killing, raping and robbing Lydia Lawson. His mother had not told him who the victim was. The name sounded familiar. He wondered if she could be related to Lawson. He was allowed to see Justin after a long wait. He entered a room separated by glass from his son. As each picked up a phone receiver on separate sides of the glass wall, they observed the painful facial expression of each. Justin spoke first and said that he did not do it, that this was a mistake, and that he did not know the person that he was accused of killing. His father assured him that he believed him and that he would get him out of jail as soon as possible. He told him that he would spare no expense and would find the best attorney available to defend him.

The next day at two-thirty in the afternoon Justin was arraigned and pleaded not guilty to all charges. He was represented by a renowned criminal defense attorney that was recommended by Bernie. The attorney's name was Art Quinn of the firm Odom Quinn & Yan, Attorneys at Law. Quinn and Bernie had been fellow law students. Although Quinn was an average student in law school, during his 25 years of practicing criminal law, he was known as a tough litigator who had never lost a case. Over the past five years many of his cases were settled before trial because of his reputation. During the arraignment, he told the judge that his client was not a flight risk; that he was a young man with a bright future ahead of him, and who had no history of criminal behavior or even of disciplinary issues, as was attested to by his teachers. He said that Justin had been accepted to Harvard and was planning to attend classes beginning in the fall. The prosecutor argued that the severity of the crime warranted that the accused remain incarcerated pending trial. "We have an eye witness account that puts him at the scene of the crime." He argued that the victim was from a prominent family that should not be forced to tolerate his freedom and be burdened with the risk of his flight. He asked that no bail be granted. After listening to the defense attorney and prosecutor, the judge ruled that no bail would be granted. A trial date was set for nine months later.

Chapter 7 - Lock-up

Justin was escorted from the court house to a waiting patrol car that would transport him back to the county jail. During the short ride back to jail, he was horrified thinking that he could be thrown away to rot in prison or put to death for a crime that he did not commit. Although he had learned at the arraignment the identity of the victim, he did not know her. He struggled to not believe that all his dreams and hard work to make them reality were now disappearing before his eyes. He had spent his young life achieving high grades, avoiding any disciplinary issues, and enjoying the closeness of his family. The thought of seeing his family from behind a glass wall or behind the walls of prison was more than he could bear. He wondered would his strength last, would his heart stop as his vision of the future was vanishing.

An hour after he returned to his cell, he was told that he had some visitors. He was led to the visiting room where he could see his father waiting behind the glass partition. As Justin walked towards him, his father picked up the receiver. He sat down, picked up the receiver, shook his head and wiped away the tears that were welling up in his eyes. "Dad, why is this happening to me? Why? I don't even know this woman that they say I killed ... I can't make it in here. It is so hard to breathe. I feel like my heart is going to explode."

His father was experiencing the same. He knew of the shortness of breath and of the erratic heartbeats that made breathing even more difficult. His body had begun reacting this way the moment he was told of Justin's arrest. He knew that he had to be strong for his son, to help him through this unjust and cruel situation. He would not show the horror and humiliation that he was enduring. He would somehow find the strength to give Justin the courage to bravely face what the future would bring. He knew that it would be ugly and could get nasty. Justin did not know, but his father knew who the victim was. She was the daughter of the man who had victimized his family many years earlier. She was Lawson's daughter, his only child... the same Lawson who had duped and robbed him of his first home. Although Justin did not know either him or her, his father knew that the prosecution would likely paint a picture of revenge during trial. He dared to think that his son's innocence could be forfeited for what could be taken as a revenge killing, regardless of evidence to the contrary. He would spare no expense to find evidence exonerating his son. To him, there was nothing more precious than family. His boy needed him and he would not fail him, no matter the cost.

"Son, look-a-here, we are gonna get through this. I know it's not right, but we gotta be strong. You gotta be strong. You gotta be strong. You have to figure out how to relax. Slow your mind down. Know in your heart that you are gonna be alright. Keep it in your heart. Tell yourself it is gonna be alright. You know that you did not do it. I know that you did not do it. We are gonna prove it. I don't know how, but we are gonna prove it. I got the best attorney in the state on the case. He ain't never lost. He gonna find a way of getting you out of here. He got people investigating this. They will find the truth. I just need for you to keep it together... keep it together... just keep it together. I love you, son. I love you. Mom and grandma are waiting to visit with you. They will only let one of us visit at a time. I am going out so they can visit. You keep it together with them. They are taking this pretty hard, especially your mom. I will be back later this week. I love you. It's gonna be alright."

Justin raised his head and said, "Dad, I love you too. I will be strong." His father's presence and spoken words had given him courage, though the fear still lingered. As he left, Justin felt the comfort and confidence of a five-year-old boy holding his father's hand. He would somehow summon the strength necessary to manage the first major crisis of his life. But he knew that he would not have to do it alone.

James motioned for the attending officer in the visiting area indicating that his visit was over. "Finished already?" James nodded yes. He had visited only about fifteen minutes to allow time for his wife and mother to see Justin before visiting hours were over. James went to the restroom as his wife began her visit with Justin. Upon entering the room, he quickly glanced around to see if anyone was there, then doubled over holding his stomach, let out a big breath and began breathing in and out heavily. A minute or so later he walked over to the sink to wash away the tears that had enveloped his cheeks. The words that he had spoken to Justin were inspirational and instructive, but at that moment, he himself drew no courage from them. Instead they overwhelmed him with emotions. He was desperately in search of hope; although he was confident that his legal team (thanks to his employer) would leave no stone unturned. Still he worried. How could he manage his days with his son locked up and in such pain?

Waiting for trial and in between visits from family and his legal team, Justin wrote letters to his sister and brother. His brother had joined the Air Force after graduating high school and was stationed on a battle ship in an unknown location. Letters to him were addressed to a Washington, D.C. address. Over the past couple of years his location changed often so Justin received only two letters in response to the four that he had sent to Cleo. The letters between Linda and Justin were sent and received monthly. She was attending a university on the East coast where she enjoyed campus life and living in the dormitory. She was doing well academically and socially. Her letters were always uplifting. She encouraged him to look beyond his present circumstances and to see that things would work out for the better. She wrote that his incarceration would soon be over and that he would be able to positively use it later in a yet unknown way. Her letters, along with family visits, motivated him not to give up. Justin began busying himself watching the news and reading the newspaper to stay apprised of current events. When he was not thinking of his fight for justice, he deeply pondered local and world events in the media. He wrote some of his thoughts down in a tablet provided to him by his grandmother:

Tell it like it is. Our world is burning with hostility; people hating people, people killing people; man-made illness, incurable disease; have mercy Lord as we fall down on our knees, and tell it like it is. Children are starving, they have no food; parents are hopeless, they cannot cope; no hope for tomorrow, life is cheap; prosperity and dignity are out of reach; just tell it like it is. Unnatural disasters, guns, missiles, drones; fighting and killing for power and greed; wildfires, mudslides, unseasonal storms; nature is master of everyone; just tell it like it is. My brother and sister, let's learn to love; no more hurting and killing, let's live in peace; mother and father take a stand; compassion and sympathy are in your hands; just tell it like it is.

Chapter 8 - Judgment Day

"Your Honor, the prosecution will now call Jonath Sinclair," the prosecuting attorney confidently says as he shuffles through papers on his table.

"Please, proceed with your next witness," the judge replies.

Sinclair steps forward and approaches the witness stand and sits down. He is casually dressed in black slacks, a blue turtle neck shirt and black loafers. He smiles as he is instructed to raise his hands as the bailiff says, "Do you solemnly swear that the testimony you are about to give will be the truth, and nothing but the truth?"

"I do."

The prosecutor, dressed in a grey suit, white shirt, and blue tie, walks slowly toward the witness. "Now sir, your name is Jonath E. Sinclair?"

"Yes, sir"

"And the E stands for Ely, is that correct?"

"Yes, but I go by El, just like the letter in the alphabet. You know, H-I-J-K-L."

"Ok, thank you, sir. Do you reside at 431 South Winter Street, Feltonia, Washington?"

"Yes, sir, I been living there for the last seven years."

"Is that a house or apartment, sir?"

"It's an apartment."

"How many apartment units are there where you live?"

"Sixteen, I think."

"And what is the name of the apartments?"

"Shady Cove"

"Do you know your neighbors in the apartments?"

"Some of them I know."

"Is your unit between other apartments or on the end?"

"I have a neighbor on each side."

"What are the addresses for the neighboring units?"

"I'm 431, so they are 430 and 432."

"Do you know the neighbor in 430?"

"Yes, his name is Mike Brown."

"What about the neighbor in 432?"

"Yes, that's Joaquim Alvarez."

"Mr. Alvarez is the current tenant, correct?"

"Yes"

"Who was the tenant before him, if you know?"

"Um, yes, that would have been Lydia Lawson. She lived there before him."

"When did she stop residing at the apartment?"

"That would have been around the end of March last year."

"Ok, let's go back to last year, March 28, 2013. Were you at home that evening between 7:00pm and 9:00pm?"

"Yes, sir, I was home watching TV. I rented a movie after work, and I was home watching it from about 6:30pm to 8:45pm."

"So, the movie ended about 8:45. What did you do after that?"

"I surfed the net for a couple of hours before going to bed."

"Ok, the movie, what was the name of it?"

"Gladiators to Super Heroes"

"Did you watch it straight through, that is, without any breaks or interruptions?"

"No, sir, I stopped a couple of times for about 10 or 15 minutes. I heard Lydia talking to somebody in front of her door, and I went out to say hello. I made some small talk with her for a few minutes."

"Lydia, do you mean Lydia Lawson?"

"Yes, sir"

"The person that she was talking to, was it a man or woman?"

"A man, a black man"

"Did you speak with him?"

"No, sir"

"Was that kind of awkward for you; you know, carrying on a conversation with her while he was standing there?"

"No, sir, as I approached them he was on his cell phone and he stepped away while Lydia and I talked."

"Well, what happened after that?"

"Nothing, I said goodbye, and went back to finish my movie."

"What did Ms. Lawson and her friend do?"

"As I was leaving, they went into her apartment."

"So, you went back to finish the movie. Did you stop watching it again later that night? You know, did you take another break?"

"Yes, sir, I did, about an hour later. Oh, it was about 8:15pm. I heard Lydia and this guy arguing. I looked out my window saw his foot in her door. She was telling him to remove it, and kept saying it was over."

"Sir, your apartment does not face hers, does it?"

"No, sir"

"How could you see his foot in her door?"

"Well, I guess I did not see it, but I heard Lydia saying get your foot out of my door."

"Were those her exact words?"

"Get your foot out of my door were her exact words."

"Do you recall approximately how many times she said, 'Get your foot out of my door,' sir?"

"I don't know exactly. She could have said it as many as 10 times. She kept saying that it was over."

"Do you know what 'It is over' meant?"

"I took it to mean that she and this guy were breaking up. I thought that he must have been her boyfriend."

The prosecutor walks back to his table to confer with his co-counsel. He and she converse as they look over their notes.

"Are you through with this witness counsel?" asks the judge.

"Your Honor, I am nearly through-- just a couple of more questions."

"Mr. Sinclair, about how long were Ms. Lawson and friend keeping you from your movie?"

"About 5 minutes"

"Were you able to see where he went?"

"No, I did not see him leave because he would have had to walk by my window."

"So, you did not see him leave, correct?"

"No, sir, I did not."

"Do you see the man that was with Ms. Lawson that night in court today?"

"Yes, I do, him," pointing at Justin Waters. "He was with her."

"Let the record show that witness Jonath Sinclair has identified the defendant Justin Waters."

"Ok, thank you, Mr. Sinclair."

"Your Honor, the prosecution is through with this witness."

"Court is in recess until 10:30am. When we resume, the defense may then cross examine the witness," the judge says and then strikes the gavel.

"All rise," says the bailiff as the judge stands and leaves the room.

Quinn was pleased with the testimony of Sinclair. There were no unpleasant surprises. He had prepared to discredit him to create doubt of Justin's guilt. As was his custom, he had thoroughly investigated Sinclair. He knew that Lydia Lawson had rejected Sinclair. She had refused a number of his romantic gestures. He had a witness that would corroborate his advances and Lawson's rejection of him. Sinclair's testimony had caused him to re-think his cross-examination strategy. He would question him about his reliability to identify his client. He would have to explain why he thought "the friend" was Lawson's boyfriend. He would have to answer questions regarding other possible exits from Lawson's apartment. Quinn thought that if he applied enough pressure on Sinclair to make him come unglued or to appear as cold and calculating in front of the jury, the prosecution would be prone to dismissing the case.

"All rise." Everyone stands while the judge walks to his seat and sits.

"Mr. Sinclair, you may now take the witness stand. I remind you that you are still under oath," says the judge.

"Mr. Quinn, is the defense ready to cross?"

"Yes, Your Honor, we are prepared to cross Mr. Sinclair,"

responds Quinn.

"Proceed"

"Good morning, Mr. Sinclair, you understand that you are still under oath?"

Sinclair raises his eyebrows and quietly says, "Yes, sir, I know."

"Sir, how well did you know Lydia Lawson?"

"Pretty good"

"Would you say that she was a friend?"

"No, not really, just a good neighbor—I would call her an acquaintance."

"Would you say that she was a lover?"

"Objection, foundation!" the prosecutor loudly calls out.

"Your Honor, may we approach?"

"Approach," the judge beckons.

The two prosecuting attorneys and Quinn walk to the judge's seat. They quietly engage in conversation. They return to their respective tables. The prosecutors appear disturbed in contrast to Quinn's neutral demeanor. He resumes his questioning of Sinclair.

"Mr. Sinclair, were you Lydia Lawson's lover?"

"No, sir, neighbors only"

"Did you ever tell anyone that you were her lover?"

"Absolutely not! Never!"

"Ok, how long were you and her acquaintances?"

"About three years"

"Where did you first meet her?"

"At Shady Cove when she moved in"

"So, are you saying that she was your neighbor for three years?"

"Yes, sir"

"During that three-year period, were the two of you ever more than acquaintances?"

"No, just good neighbors"

"Ok, did you on one or more occasions ever pursue a romantic relationship with Ms. Lawson?"

"No! We were just neighbors." Sinclair begins fidgeting in his seat.

"So, is it your testimony that you never sought a romantic relationship with Ms. Lawson?"

"Objection, Your Honor; asked and answered," the prosecutor stands up and looks toward the judge.

"Move on, Mr. Quinn," the judge replies.

"You stated that you thought 'the friend' with Ms. Lawson on the night of March 28th was her boyfriend. Please explain why."

"He was with her, and I heard her say that it was over?"

"Did you hear her say exactly what 'it' was? Did she say

exactly what was over?"

"No, I did not hear that."

"So, could she have meant the end of a friendship?"

"Yes, sir"

"Could she have meant the end of a project?

"Yes, sir"

"So, could 'it is over' have meant any number of things?"

"Yes, sir," reaching in his trousers to get a handkerchief to wipe the sweat from his forehead.

"Did you see them hold hands?"

"No, sir"

"Did you see them hugging?"

"No, sir"

"Did you see them kiss?"

"No, sir"

"Had you ever seen him before that night?"

"No, sir"

"Mr. Sinclair, do you know Janice Louis?"

"Yes, I do"

"How do you know Ms. Louis?"

"She was Lydia's roommate for a year or so."

"Ok, do you know Henry Dennerson?"

"Yes"

"Who is he?"

"A friend, I've known him since grade school."

"Ok, let's go back to Janice Louis, Ms. Lawson's roommate. Do you recall making regular visits to Ms. Lawson's apartment while Ms. Louis roomed with her?"

"I wouldn't say regular, but I did visit a few times."

"Do you recall during Ms. Louis' stay there that Ms. Lawson asked you to leave her apartment?"

"No, I was never asked to leave."

"Ok, let's go on to your friend, Henry Dennerson. Do you recall telling him that you were interested in Ms. Lawson romantically?"

"No, I do not"

"Are you saying that you do not recall or that you deny it ever happened?"

"Sir, I deny it ever happened. I was not interested in her that way."

"Do you recall telling your friend that you had slept with Ms. Lawson?"

"No, absolutely not!" now squirming in his seat, "Absolutely not!"

"And do you recall Ms. Lawson confronting you because of a rumor that you were sleeping with her?"

"No, she never said anything to me about that kind of rumor."

"Alright, let's go back to the night of March 28, 2013, between the hours of 7:00pm to 9:00pm. Your testimony is that you met Ms. Lawson and her friend in the front of her apartment, correct?"

"Yes, sir, that's right."

"You testified that her friend was a black man, correct?"

"Yes, sir"

"About how tall was he?"

"I don't know exactly."

"Well, did he look like he was your height, taller or shorter?"

"I didn't see him up close, and it was dark. I'd say he was about 5'11" or 6'."

"How tall are you?"

"Five feet and nine inches"

"So, you're saying that you could tell he was taller than you?"

"Yes, sir, he was"

"His weight, about how much would you say he weighed?"

"I don't know."

"How much do you weigh?"

"About 175"

"So, did he look like he was about your weight?"

"Oh no, he looked much heavier—maybe 20 to 30 pounds or so."

"What kind of clothes was he wearing?"

"I think he had on blue jeans, a red short-sleeved shirt and sneakers."

"The black man that you described is about 5'11" to 6', much heavier than 175 pounds and talking on a cell phone all the while you are making small talk with Ms. Lawson. Is that correct?"

"Yes, sir"

"While he was on his cell were you able to see any piercings or tattoos?"

"No, it was dark."

"Did you hear any of his conversation?"

"No, he was talking softly and at a distance."

"You did not notice any piercings, tattoos and you never heard his voice. Is that correct?"

"Correct, yes"

"Did you ever see his full face? That is to say, his face when he was not on the cell phone?"

"No, sir, he stayed on the cell phone."

"Did you notice any facial hair?"

"No, sir"

"No beard? No mustache?"

"Asked and answered," says the prosecutor.

"Ok, I'll move on. You said earlier that you never saw the man leave Ms. Lawson's, correct?"

"Yes, sir, that's right."

"You said that he would have had to pass by your window, correct?"

"Correct"

"Could he have left without your noticing; say while you surfed the net?"

"No, sir, my computer is next to the window, and I opened my blinds after I heard them arguing. I left them open until I went to bed."

"What time did you go to bed?"

"About 11:15pm"

"Is your bed next to the window?"

"No, sir"

"Where is your bed?"

"In the back bedroom"

"Would you have been able to see him leave from your bedroom?"

"No, sir"

"Why is that?"

"Because it is in the back away from the front sidewalks where he would have had to leave"

"Ok, does your bedroom have a window?"

"Yes, sir"

"What is outside of the window?"

"An open green area"

"Is it fenced in?"

"No, sir"

"Was there anything in the back area that would keep a person from leaving the apartments?"

"No, sir"

"Earlier you said that you visited Ms. Lawson's apartment in the past. Can you describe the floor plan of her apartment?"

"Yes, it is identical to mine. It is a two-bedroom unit with a living room, kitchen, and small dining room off the kitchen. They are up front and the bedrooms are in the back."

"So, would it be possible for someone to exit from either bedroom window and leave the apartments?

"Yes, sir, I guess so."

"Let me try to sum up what your testimony is. If I make a mistake, please correct me. You saw a black man in the dark on a cell phone; you never heard his voice; you did not notice any facial hair, piercings, or tattoos; you never saw him leave, but he could have left from a back bedroom window without you noticing. Is that correct?"

"Yes, sir"

"Thank you, Mr. Sinclair."

"Your Honor, the defense is through with this witness."

"The prosecution may now re-direct," says the judge.

The prosecutor responds, "We are through with this witness, Your Honor."

"Is the defense ready to put on its witnesses?"

Quinn stands and says, "May we approach the bench, Your Honor?"

"Would this be a brief matter for discussion? If not, I will dismiss court for today, do it in chambers and resume tomorrow," the judge says while looking at the jurors.

Justin had sat listening to Sinclair being questioned by the prosecution and the defense. There was something familiar about him but he could not put his finger on it. He did not know him and was not aware of ever meeting him, yet there was something about his face that haunted him. He searched the depths of his mind to find out why he had such an impression of him. Listening to his voice in response to the questions did not help. Only during Quinn's questioning of his alleged affair with Lydia Lawson did Justin grasp where their paths had crossed. It was on the night of the school concert. Justin, before going to the concert, went to a Red Box kiosk outside a major grocery store a few blocks from the school. He wanted to rent a movie to watch after the concert. While there he had to wait on one person in front of him to complete his transaction at the kiosk. The person kept looking back at him as he waited. Justin noticed that each time he looked back his eyes would wander. He became annoyed at what he thought was excessive time at the kiosk. "Sir, are you familiar with how to use the kiosk?" Sinclair turned around, looked at him and said nervously, "Yes, I'm just about done."

Justin thought that Quinn should know. He lightly tapped him on his shoulder as Quinn finished his response to the judge. "No, Your Honor, I do not believe it will be brief. And I think justice will be better served in chambers."

"Mr. Quinn, I really need to speak with you." He then told him how he was familiar with Sinclair.

Chapter 9 - Circling the Wagons

It was now about 3:30 on a hotter than usual afternoon and the jurors had sat through five days of court listening to the prosecution put on its case against the defendant with testimony from prosecution witnesses. Two of the most notable were Jonath Sinclair who identified Justin as the murderer, and Alex Lawson to imply motive. Through the testimony of Lawson, the prosecution tried to show that Justin took revenge on Lawson by raping, robbing and murdering his daughter. Lawson testified that his company had acquired Justin's family home 12 years earlier for default on a loan. His parents had come to his office in protest and left threatening to put him out of business. He testified that the boy was only about 5 years old at the time but was with his father when he signed for the loan. After the defense's objection for relevance was overruled, Lawson was allowed to comment on the parent's state of mind at the time as combative and menacing.

The prosecution's star witness, Sinclair, was the only person who claimed to have put Justin at the scene of the crime. He identified him in lock-up when Justin, along with five other suspects, was placed behind a glass partition for him to identify. All the suspects were black. Justin was the youngest, and this was his first time behind bars. He was nervous and visibly shaken; his eyes wandered errantly as he was given instructions by the jailer: "Step forward; face right; face left; place your right hand to your ear; place your left hand to your ear." The others, who had been in lock-up on previous occasions, comfortably followed the instructions without showing any sign of distress. Sinclair chose Justin.

Justin had spent just over nine months in jail before his trial. His mother, father and grandmother did not let a day pass without paying him a visit. They rotated visits to ensure that at least one family member would see him every day. His sister Linda, away in college, wrote to him each month. He wrote her back each time. Writing was one of his ways of coping with his time behind bars. It relieved some of the emotional pressure that he battled daily. With the passing of time, daily visits, letter writing and continuous prayer, Justin dared to take some degree of comfort—courage to hope and believe that the nightmare would end soon. Though he could never understand how and why this could happen to him. He questioned why he was not released after the prosecution received a sworn statement that he was performing in a school band concert across town from 6:30pm to 8:00pm. He continued to question it even though his attorney told him that the prosecution believed that he had an hour to go across town to commit the crimes. (The defense did not believe that he had time to do so.) Each night before closing his eyes, and when awaking each morning, he would pray for freedom.

Chapter 10 - Misidentification

In the judge's chamber, Quinn asked that the case be dismissed based on insufficient evidence; his client was misidentified. He pointed to the inconsistencies of Sinclair's testimony.

"Mr. Sinclair should not be considered a credible witness as a matter of law. The factual basis on which he uses to describe my client clearly exonerates him. He says that Ms. Lawson's friend was 5'11" to 6'. My client is 5'6". Even if you argue that he was confused, he says that the person was taller than 5'9". How does he know that? Because he is five nine, and that person was taller than him. What of the person's weight? He says that he was at least 195 pounds. Remember, he says the person was some 20 to 30 pounds heavier than him. He weighs 175. As to a facial description, he says it was too dark to see him. He could not provide a single descriptive marker of his face or body. He says that he did not see any piercings or tattoos. What exactly did he see? Well, I think it is clear. He saw whatever his imagination could conjure up. His imagination, what about it? 'It is over,' those words he says were repeated a number of times by Ms. Lawson. He uses his imagination, not facts, to tell you what they mean. He says that they meant Ms. Lawson and he were breaking up as a couple. Yet when questioned he admits that he never saw them hold hands, hug, or kiss. In fact, he had never seen this guy before. I have witnesses who will testify that Mr. Sinclair had a romantic interest in Ms. Lawson, and that he spread a rumor that he was sleeping with her."

Months earlier, a Quinn investigator had found Lydia Lawson's former roommate, Janice Louis, now Janice Dennerson; she took the last name of her husband, Henry (Hank) Dennerson. The investigator had learned that Hank, whom she was dating, while still a roommate to Lydia Lawson, told her that Jonath Sinclair was sleeping with her roommate. Assuming it to be true, one evening Janice shared with Lydia what Hank told her. Lydia denied it and became very upset. That evening as Sinclair returned home from work Lydia invited him over. He went over after showering and dousing himself in cologne. This was the moment he had been waiting for. Almost immediately, as he sat on the living room sofa, Janice said, "How are you doing, Jonath?" He said, "I'm doing real good," looking at Lydia, "How are you girls?" Janice smiled and said, "You are pretty smooth. How long have you and Lydia been seeing each other?" Trying to avoid Lydia's glare, he looked away and said, "Oh, no, we are just good neighbors." Lydia, not able to remain silent any longer, "Why are you telling people that we are sleeping together? You know that it is not true. The only times that you and I have ever been in the same room together another person has always been with us. Why are you spreading these lies?" Standing up and slowly walking towards the front door, Sinclair said, "I have never told anybody that." Janice, "So, are you saying that you

71

did not tell Hank that you were 'tapping' that? And 'to keep it a secret' because she does not want anybody to know?' Is he lying?" Sinclair stood still as though paralyzed, speechless and his eyes shifted erratically from left to right, up and down. Lydia yelled, "Get out! Get out! You disgust me!"

The investigator had also separately interviewed Henry Dennerson. His account of the events verified his wife's statements. The only difference was that her husband recalled the actual words used by Sinclair. Because of the graphic way he described the sexual relationship with Lydia, the husband did not believe him. Also, he did not believe him because he knew when Sinclair was lying. Since sixth grade, he had observed Sinclair's eyes wandering and a choppy speech pattern when he was lying.

The judge and the prosecution listened intently to Quinn until he paused and looked at the judge. He then continued.

"Your Honor, I believe that it would be a great miscarriage of justice to allow this trial to move forward. My client, a 4.0 student and model citizen by all accounts, has been locked up over 9 months for crimes that he could not have possibly committed. With the evidence that we have from the prosecution's star witness and sworn statements from my client's school band director and fellow students that he was across town in a performance from 6:30 to 8:00 on the night of the crimes, show that he could not have possibly done them. If the case is not dismissed, I am prepared to offer testimony that further disproves the prosecution's case, and further puts in question the credibility of the prosecution's chief witness. My client is innocent of all charges, and I request that he be released immediately."

Quinn stops speaking and there is a moment of silence. The judge then clears his throat, looks at the prosecuting attorneys, and then says, "What is the prosecution's position on this?"

"Your Honor, Mr. Quinn has brought to our attention some facts that were previously unknown in the aggregate. He questions the reliability of our witness, and has given us reason to pause. We have to agree that it does not appear that the defendant could have committed the crimes. The prosecution would be amenable to dismissing the charges forthwith against his client. But I would like Mr. Quinn to facilitate our dialogue with his proposed witnesses, and the prosecution will re-visit our review of Mr. Sinclair, and in particular his involvement with Ms. Lydia Lawson. We would like to do whatever is necessary to solve the crimes against Ms. Lawson. We certainly do not wish to punish an innocent person."

Back in court the following day at 8:00AM. The judge walks to his seat while the bailiff (facing the court audience) says, "All rise." The judge sits, turns to the jury, and begins speaking.

"Ladies and gentlemen of the Jury, thank you for your time and sacrifice. The court has reviewed the facts of this case and closely considered the testimonies and arguments alleging guilt of the defendant. I am hereby dismissing all charges against Mr. Justin Waters. A review of the testimony and documentation clearly show that there is no evidence supporting the allegations against him. It is clear that the witness who identified him had no substantial basis for doing so. In summary, he testifies that he saw a black man on the phone in the dark, and provided no facial recognition description. The description of his body height and weight conflicts with that of the defendant. I am hereby moving that defendant Justin Waters be released immediately and without delay. Ladies and gentlemen of the jury, the court once again thanks you."

At the moment that the judge said Justin was to be released his mother let out a muffled scream (her hands clasped over her mouth) and with tears flowing down her cheeks, looked up and whispered, "Thank you, Jesus." Justin's mother, father and grandmother stood up and began to hug each other while wiping the tears from their eyes.

Tapping his gavel, the judge, "Court is hereby adjourned."

Chapter 11 - Late Harvest

Janice, scratching her head then placing her thumb on her cheek bone and index finger on her chin, softly said, "Lydia told me that she met a guy (an older guy) that interested her romantically. She said that she met him on the college campus, and at first, she thought he was a professor but he was a retired student counselor. She said he was tall, dark and distinguished looking. The guy was her father's age or older so she was not anxious to introduce him to her father. She said that she was not sure how her dad would react." Looking up slowly, turning her head slightly and after taking a deep breath, "The truth is I don't think it was an age thing." Quinn had facilitated an interview with Janice Dennerson for the prosecutor's office. Janice was now being interviewed by a woman from the office.

The woman asked Janice why she did not believe it was an "age thing." Janice went on to explain that she met the guy one afternoon when she was on campus. "This guy was very charming and educated. I was seated next to him in the student restaurant. He was with three or four young black students whom he was advising on how to get a well-rounded education. He was giving them very good advice. When the students left for class he invited himself to my table. It made me a bit uncomfortable but I thought what's the harm? We're in a public place and he will see my wedding ring and that will be that.

75

But boy was I ever wrong. Suffice it to say, he asked for my phone number after a number of inappropriate questions and comments. A few days later when I was back on campus again I saw him with Lydia as I was parking." The woman from the prosecutor's office stopped typing and looked up from her laptop, "Are you sure it was the same guy?" Nodding her head yes, Janice said, "It certainly was. Lydia had mentioned that he had a scar in the shape of a half-moon above his left eye. So did this guy. And if I had any doubt, it left when I saw him kiss her."

The woman again looked up from her keyboard and asked, "Did you get his name?"

"Yes, not the last name but I remember him saying Jake, and I remember the students calling him 'Mr. Jay'." Clearing her throat, the woman continues, "You said Lydia thought that he was very distinguished looking. Did you find that to be so? And if so, in what way?"

"He was, I guess," Janice paused, and glancing into the distance continued, "a black man with dark skin and a short afro that looked to be about three inches long (that I think was dyed because it was so shiny), a salt and pepper mustache and beard that was nicely trimmed. He also wore these black plastic glasses that looked like they were from an earlier time, maybe the sixties."

"What about his clothing?" asked the woman. "Oh, nothing

particularly noteworthy—blue jeans, black sneakers and a blue sweatshirt."

"Do you know if Lydia was sexually active with this guy?" Janice sat up straight and rested her chin in her opposite hand. "You know, I don't know. Something didn't seem right about the guy being with her. I'd like to think that she eventually saw him the way I saw him."

"One last question, you said that he was tall. How tall?"

"Oh," looking upward Janice said, "I would say he was at least six-one, maybe a little taller even."

****

Mike Brown, a resident of Shady Cove, had lived in apartment 430 for the past 10 years. He worked as a city bus driver and was a personal fitness trainer in his spare time. He worked a10-hour shift from four-thirty in the morning to two-thirty in the afternoon or from two-thirty to twelve-thirty in the morning. He was a workout junkie and was very muscular from his time spent lifting weights. Regardless of his shift, he worked out daily at a 24-hour fitness center near him. He would go directly from work to the center and would often arrive home between four and six in the morning. Brown was now being interviewed by a man from the prosecutor's office.

"Mr. Brown, did you know your neighbor, Lydia Lawson, who

lived in apartment 432?"

"Yes, I knew her."

"How did you know her?"

"Well, I was her personal fitness trainer for several months."

"Were you aware of her friends or who came to visit her regularly?"

"Not too much...at one point she had a room-mate. I think her name was Janice. So, I'm not sure who was a friend to who. I would sometimes see her father come and visit."

"Ok, her room-mate later moved out. Did you see anybody else visiting her?"

"Uum, come to think about it, I did see a guy going over there or leaving early in the morning as I was coming home from an early morning workout or sometimes as I was leaving for work on the early shift."

"Can you describe the guy?"

"I never was up to close to him, but I know he was tall, over six feet. He had an afro and walked funny, almost with a limp."

"Did he have any facial hair, tattoos or piercings?"

"I'm not sure. I know that he did not have any sideburns but he may have had a beard or mustache. I remember now. I met him one morning as he was leaving Lydia's. His hands were cupped over his face covering his mouth, chin and most of his nose. You know, like he was in deep thought. I said, 'good morning' but he said nothing, just kept walking."

"When you met him that morning did you notice anything about his face?

"Yes, I did. There was some kind of dark mark, a scar or birthmark above one of his eyes."

"Which eye?"

"I was facing him so I'm pretty sure it was the left eye."

"What about the scar? Can you describe it?"

"It was pretty large, about as long as his eyebrow. It was shaped like a half circle."

"Where was the bottom of the circle? Was it pointing away or towards his eye?"

"It definitely pointed towards his eye. That's what made it very noticeable. His eyebrow and scar were in opposite directions."

"Do you recall the approximate date and time you met this guy?"

"It would have been in March." Scratching his head and lifting his right hand to his forehead, "Probably the last week in March since that was the same day I got a check that I had been expecting from one of my fitness clients. It was on the floor as I walked into my apartment just beneath the mail slot in the door. As to the time of morning, it was after my workout—probably about four in the morning."

* *

In March of 2011, Cleo was a senior and was exploring his options beyond high school. He considered going to a university, community college or joining the armed forces. Although he was not sure where he would land, he decided to look into community college first. He thought that he could do the first two years there then transfer to a university because it would be less expensive. He signed up for a visit to Feltonia Community College. In the third week of March he attended an orientation sponsored by the college. He toured the campus and met with staff that answered questions and sold the virtues of the college. When appropriate they referred to other recent graduates who were enrolled or who had moved on to a university after attending the college. The college provided the students with lunch in the student restaurant with faculty and a few college students to answer any additional questions and to continue selling the virtues of the college.

Lydia was among the staff chosen because of her age, just a few years older than the students. She had a very fluid interaction with the students and made them feel comfortable. She made a very deliberate attempt to learn the name of each and to always ask what made them consider going to Feltonia. She noticed among the visiting students one who had a very uncanny resemblance to Jake. He was about the same height, with no facial hair or scar above his eye, and about 20 years younger. She wanted to know if he was related to Jake so she directed a question to him. "Young man, what is your name?" Cleo responded, "Cleo Winston."

"Why are you interested in possibly attending the college? Any particular interest?"

"No, I'm just exploring all of my options. Someone suggested that I should consider the college because it would be cheaper than moving away to attend somewhere else."

"That sounds like pretty solid advice. "

****

"Mr. Sinclair, thank you for coming in today. Our office is still investigating the death of your neighbor, Lydia Lawson. We wanted to look more closely at what you may know that could help us in solving her death. As you know, you identified the wrong man at trial. But I'll try not to go over too much of what was already covered in court unless absolutely necessary for clarity, alright?" Sinclair nods yes, clears his throat and crosses his legs. "Let's talk about who you may have observed going in and out of her apartment. Did you see any individuals that visited her regularly?" Taking a sip of water from his water bottle, Sinclair uncrosses his legs, places his elbows on the table and leans in. "Her father was there pretty often, well sometimes, maybe two or three times a month. He'd usually say hi or wave to me as he was coming or going. Her friend Janice would drop in also. I can't say off hand that I remember seeing anybody else on the regular?"

"Janice? Do you mean Janice Louis (or Dennerson), her old room-mate?"

"Yes."

"Okay, those are the regular visitors. Can you recall anybody else that you saw over there that were not regular visitors?"

"I did see a tall black guy one time at her door. I never saw his face. It was about 10 o'clock one night."

"Did he go in?"

"Yes."

"When was this?"

"Shortly before she was killed?"

"What do you mean 'shortly?' When exactly?"

"It was in March, probably a week or two before she died."

"Did she seem to know him?"

"I guess so. She let him in."

"Okay. Your apartment is next to hers, and from looking at the layout, one of your bedrooms is next to one of her bedrooms, separated by a wall only. Also, your dining room is next to her living room. Could you hear the TV, radio or any conversation next door?"

"Uh, yes I could sometimes hear her music or TV."

"Music?"

"I didn't mind. I liked the music that she would play."

"And how do you know it was the TV, say and not the radio?"

"It was cable news, sometimes CNN or MSNBC. I recognized the hosts, Rachel Maddow, Don Lemon, or whoever."

"Would she have the TV volume up usually?"

"No, I think the walls are pretty thin or hollow—maybe no insulation in them because they are not external walls. I could sometimes hear my other neighbor, Mike, on the phone."

"You mean Mr. Brown, your neighbor at 430?"

"Yes, he gets in late sometimes, and I used to hear him on the phone. I told him about it so I don't hear him anymore."

"Would you say that when you did hear him that he was talking loud or yelling?"

"No, I don't think so. Just, well at that time of day (early morning) everything is quiet so nothing can drown out his voice. During the day, you hear other things that are louder, traffic, birds or even people talking loud outside."

"Getting back to Ms. Lawson, what about her music? Was the volume up when she played it?"

"Yes, probably so, at least more than the TV. I could hear her singing along with it."

"When would you hear the TV or the music? What time of day?"

"Most of the time I would hear the TV early evening, around about five to seven. The music was later. I'd hear it sometimes around eight-thirty or nine at night. Every now and then after eleven I could barely hear it."

"Did you ever hear anything else? Say when her father came over? Did you hear them talking?"

"Well, I might hear them laughing but usually not anything beyond that. Most of the time I was on YouTube, watching TV or something like that."

"So, you could hear them laughing sometimes in the living room, and sometimes in the bedroom you could hear her singing, right?"

"Um-hum, yes, sir"

"Mr. Sinclair, do you drive or own a car?"

"No, sir, I don't drive. I usually take the bus, a green thing. With a monthly bus pass, I can go anywhere in the city."

"Do you know how to drive, like say, if you were to rent a car?"

"I have never found a reason to learn, so no, I don't."

"Thank you, Mr. Sinclair, for coming in today. You have been very helpful. If you are finish with your water, I can put the bottle in our recycling bin for you."

"Yes, I'm finish. Here you go," handing the bottle over.

"Just leave it there on the table. We'll toss it for you. Have a good day."

****

"Alright, little brothers, I will see you next week. If you can't make it, call me, or if you need me before our next meeting, call." Jake watched as three first year students got up from the table and headed out of the restaurant to class. His session with them had been particularly pleasing to him, having heard one of the students say that there were other students interested in his counsel. Another had said that her academic adviser noticed that she had improved her grades dramatically and wanted to know how she did it. She told him that it was because of Jake's counsel. He finished his coffee, gathered his notes, stood up, put on his windbreaker, pushed the chair under the table and started to walk out of the restaurant.

"Mr. Masters, Jake Masters?" A man dressed in a sports coat, neck tie and denim slacks said, "Sir, do you have a moment? My name is John Oliver, and I am from the DA's office."

Hoping to begin a dialogue about future employment as a student counselor, he had first thought it was someone from the college faculty. He looked around and saw another man similarly dressed at the exit and two uniformed police officers through the glass doors standing near a patrol car. "How can I help you?" He said nervously.

"Mr. Masters, as I said, I am from the DA's office and we are looking into the death of Lydia Lawson. We are interviewing many of her acquaintances. We understand that you knew her, right? "

"Yes, I knew her."

"We would like to question you at our office? Do you mind riding with us?"

Again, looking towards the exit, "If I say not now, are those officers out there to arrest me?"

"Sir, we would rather it not come to that. At this point we just want to ask you some questions." Not wanting to make a scene, Jake reluctantly said, "Alright, I'll go with you."

"Mr. Masters, for the record we are going to record this interview." Turning on a hand-held digital recorder, Oliver presses the record button. "In the matter of the death of Lydia Lawson, interview of Jake Masters. The aforementioned spelled J-A-K-E (Jake) and M-A-S-T-E-R-S (Masters). Mr. Masters state your name for the record."

"Jake Masters"

"Please state your current address."

"29 South Harbor Rd., Feltonia, Washington"

"Did you know Lydia Lawson?"

"Yes"

"How did you come to know her?"

"I met her at Feltonia Community College about three years ago."

"What was the nature of your relationship?"

"She was my girlfriend."

"Did you know where she lived? If so, did you ever visit her there?"

"Yes, I knew her address and I would go there."

"Can you give me her address?"

"432 South Winter, Feltonia"

"What was the nature of your visits?"

"Pretty much like that of any two people who are romantically involved and would like intimacy"

"Did the intimacy include sex?"

"Sure, it did."

"When was the last time that you had sex with her?"

"The night before I found out she was killed"

"Did you attend her funeral? You know, after all, she was your girlfriend."

"No, I did not," shaking his head "because she would not have wanted me to."

"Why is that?"

"Our relationship was low key. She didn't want others to know we were seeing each other. I would usually visit her late at night and leave early in the morning."

"Did she ever not want to have sex with you but you did it anyway?"

"No, I would not force myself on her! If she didn't want it we didn't do it."

"Did you ever punch, kick or in any other way physically abuse her?"

"Hell no! What is this?"

"Mr. Masters, settle down please. So, you never hurt her, right?"

"That's right. We had consensual sex."

"Didn't it upset you that she wanted to keep your relationship secret?"

"A little bit but I did not mind so much after I thought it through because I was trying to get a job with the college. She was watching out for any openings that would interest me."

"Going back to your last night with her, what else did you do that night besides having sex?"

"We went to a late-night movie on the other side of town. We didn't want to run into people who knew us."

"What did you watch and which theater?"

"I don't remember because it wasn't about the movie, just wanted to get out of the apartment. Anyway, I paid for it with my credit card. Two tickets, one for me and one for her along with some snacks are on my card."

"Do you still use that card?"

"Yes, I do. Am I allowed to ask questions of you?"

"You have a question?"

"Yes. I heard that Lydia was raped and robbed. I did not rape her but she probably was not robbed."

"Why do you say that, Mr. Masters?"

"Well, answering your question about the movie reminds of something that I am not proud of but may help you with the investigation. Unless whoever killed her took something other than her wallet and credit cards, I don't think she was robbed. You see, she left her purse with her wallet and credit cards at my house. I still have them. I'm sure you did not find any trace of the cards being used because they are at my house. I could not return them to anybody because our relationship was private. I know she talked about her dad sometimes but I don't think she wanted him to know about me."

Chapter 12 - Altered Landscaping

A year had passed since the death of Lydia Lawson. An accusation and trial of the wrong man had sent a stern message to the DA resulting in the election of a new DA. The case was now being reviewed from top to bottom. The coroner's office was instructed to look at all the evidence again and a new legal team was assigned to the case. The new DA had campaigned on a theme of competent justice for victims of crime. She had painted a picture of her opponent as eager incompetence at work. She had used the plight of Justin Waters, his nine-month deprivation of freedom for a crime that he did not do, to say that Justin was an innocent victim of the former DA's failure in carrying out the duties of the office. She held him up as an ideal young man with a promising future that had been unnecessarily derailed. She had pledged to not only review the case and to leave no stone unturned but would also review other pending and old cases to make sure that the innocent were not prosecuted. The coroner's office sent over its report to the DA with a cover letter stating that there were no new findings. The report showed that Lydia Lawson had died of strangulation. The photos showed bruising around her neck and on her inner thighs (thought to be from the knees of the abuser to pry open her legs). It also showed the left side of her face along the jaw line protruding. Her jaw had been broken by what appeared to be the result of a right-hand punch. There were trace amounts of skin and hair found in her right hand under her fingernails (index finger and thumb) and soap residue on both hands. There was semen and skin cells found in her vagina from two different donors. And there were skin cells collected from the bruise on her face and around her neck. She had been dead no more than four hours before being found.

The Feltonia police detective in charge had been asked to review his report and to meet with the lead investigator for the DA. The police had arrived on the scene after receiving a call from Lydia Lawson's father. He and his daughter had scheduled an early morning breakfast but when he arrived to pick her up, she did not answer the door when he rang the doorbell. The light was on in the living room so he thought that she was waiting on him and would open immediately. He thought maybe she was in the bathroom. He rang again but no answer. He had seen her car in the parking lot on his way to her apartment so she had to be there. He waited a few minutes then called her cell. No answer. Lawson hung up and dialed 911. A police officer arrived at 7:03 AM, about 20 minutes after the call. He rang the doorbell but when he got no answer he knocked hard on the door. Still no answer. He awoke the on-sight manager and told him to unlock the door. Inside, they heard the shower running in the bathroom. The father called out her name as he entered, slowly pushing back the door, gasping at the heat, and removing his glasses that had quickly fogged up from the fog. He stepped in, pulled the curtain back and turned off the water. Meanwhile the police called out "Ms. Lawson" as he opened the door of the bedroom closest to the bathroom. She was there, lying face up on the bed, not moving.

The police investigation unit had arrived at the apartment at 7:51AM. They sealed off the crime scene and spent the next four hours processing the apartment. Most of the time was spent in the South bedroom where the victim lay until 10:00AM when the coroner's office took her. The lead detective was careful to preserve the scene with plenty of photos. On the bed, he observed dry stains and some wet substance about a quarter of an inch wide and three inches long. It was semen. He gathered the sheets and other bedding, placing them in separate bags for the crime lab. Under the bed, he found a bus ticket which he dusted for fingerprints before placing it in an envelope. The unit dusted all doors for fingerprints. Back at the lab they discovered that none of the prints on the front door were those of Lydia Lawson, only those of the responding officer and apartment manager, and on the bathroom door those of Mr. Lawson, and those of the police officer on the South bedroom door. All other doors in the apartment had Lydia Lawson's prints on them. On the headboard in the bedroom and bathroom sink faucets, in addition to her prints, there were another set of prints. They would later be determined to be those of Jake Masters.

Earlier in the week Jonath Sinclair and Jake Masters had been interviewed by the DA, Jake as a suspect and Sinclair, a potential witness. Jake was a suspect based on evidence at the crime scene and the observations of others. As a felon, having served time for manslaughter, his prints and DNA were in the State's criminal database. He had admitted to knowing the victim, having sex with her and to having possession of her property. He had denied abusing her or killing her but the evidence was stacked against him. Sinclair, on the other hand, was not under any suspicion. The DA was considering using him as one of several witnesses against Jake. To avoid being blind-sided, they decided to eliminate him from any possible connection to the prints found in the apartment. He had been coaxed into leaving his water bottle on the table, which was later dusted for prints and sent to the lab for comparison with those of the bus ticket. They were identical. They belonged to Sinclair.

Sinclair was arrested on the job that afternoon. The DA now had a reasonable basis for searching his apartment and to get his DNA. They did not know what they would find in the apartment but his DNA could be linked to the skin under Lydia Lawson's fingernails and the semen from the second donor found on her bed sheet and in her. The next morning Sinclair was arraigned and pleaded not guilty to the murder and rape of Lydia Lawson. He was represented by a public defense attorney who asked for bail but was denied. As a suspect charged with a crime, Sinclair was required to give his DNA. His finger prints had put him at the scene of the crime but the DA wanted more to tie him to the rape. If his DNA was not found in the bedroom, she would drop the charges against him and charge Jake. She had a hunch that Jake was probably set up but she needed to prove it. The lab results were back. His DNA matched the semen of the unknown male. The skin from Lydia Lawson's fingernails, and cells found on her face from the punch and around her neck and in her vagina, were also a match. She had the right man. All that remained was the motive behind his crimes.

The DA, as she finished reading the report, scowled at the results on the last page. Jake's DNA was tied to a 1988 cold case that she was not familiar with. It had never been sent to the DA for prosecution. The case number was for the Feltonia Police Department. Continuing to read, she picked up her phone and called the department to request a copy of the case file. She hung up, pressed the intercom button for her secretary and told her to retrieve from archives a file on Jake who had been prosecuted for involuntary manslaughter in 1996.

Chapter 13 - *Plowed Under*

Sitting at her desk, the DA had two files to review. One was for Jake's 1996 prosecution for the death of a bar patron, and the other was for a 1988 hit-and-run case. She decided to learn as much as she could about Jake before reviewing the hit-and-run. She thought it might give her a clue for what to look for in the other.

In 1996, Jake had been found guilty of involuntary manslaughter. He was thirty-three years old at the time. He had been released after serving three years. The manslaughter conviction against him was for the death of a man in a bar room brawl. That night, around mid-night, Jake had been drinking since about six in the evening. He had come to the bar alone, but he and various patrons that came and went had engaged in friendly conversations. The more he drank the more critical he became of others. Many had slowly eased away from him to avoid confrontation. One man sat drinking at the bar unaware of what others had observed of Jake. He would slowly sip his drink and look straight ahead, appearing to be in deep thought. Jake gingerly walked over to take a seat next to him. He said hello and the man nodded hello. Jake started rambling on about this that and the other while the man looked at him and listened. Jake abruptly stopped and asked, "Is there something on my face?" The man said nothing. Jake asked again, and still the man said nothing, smiled, and looked away.

Jake, now incensed, loudly threatened to whip the man. The man looked down at his glass and raised his arm to take a sip, then Jake slammed his arm back down to the bar, saying "You think you're too good to talk to me!" With his opposite arm, the man pushed Jake away while jerking his other arm free as Jake fell from his seat to the floor. The man raised his glass to his mouth as Jake quickly got up from the floor, punched the man in his face, knocking him off his seat but not to the floor. Jake then threw an uppercut with his other arm and another punch to the jaw. The man fell to the floor, hitting his head on the corner of a table on the way down. The case was scheduled to go to trial with a charge of manslaughter. Jake pleaded not guilty, self-defense. He claimed that the man initiated the fight and that he was simply defending himself. The prosecution had numerous witnesses that would testify that Jake was the aggressor who had insulted and provoked not only the man but others also during the evening. Jake's attorney had viewed a copy of a video obtained from the bar by the prosecution showing Jake flailing his arms, head bobbing and mouth stretched wide open (no audio) as bar patrons eventually moved away from him. It showed him going over to the bar stool next to the man and all that followed. His attorney had gathered as much information about Jake's life as possible. He did not want any surprises at trial. Jake's involvement in the criminal justice system had started in his teens. He had been picked up numerous times by law enforcement, for theft, fighting, DUII and for an allegation of rape. Each time except for the DUII, the charges had been dropped. Witnesses had backed out so he was let off with a warning and was released into the custody of his parents with instructions to better monitor him. He was the ninth child of fifteen living with two working parents who struggled financially and were not able to pay any additional attention to Jake. At age sixteen, he had a baby with his 15-year old girlfriend. He had since then fathered seven more children with three other women. He was a college graduate with a BA in sociology, a master's in counseling, and he worked as a university student counselor. After viewing the video, his attorney had advised him to cop a plea, which he did, and he was given a five-year sentence.

Yes, just as she thought, Jake was more than meets the eye. She had been told by the attorneys in charge of the Lydia Lawson investigation that he was cooperative, articulate and helpful. He had admitted to having a secret intimate relationship with Lydia Lawson and to having evidence that could implicate him in the crimes against her. The question was why was he so forthcoming? Was it a ploy to deflect attention from himself? What was his angle? Or was he innocent and just wanted it all to go away? She closed the file and pushed it to the corner of her desk and grabbed the other one from the opposite corner. The label on the file read: Hit-and-Run, FPD#1177, Investigator Al Olson.

There was a two-vehicle collision in the intersection of NE Milan Street and Hanover Street at approximately 9:15AM, August 9, 1988. One vehicle was traveling West on Hanover and the other heading North on Milan. The West bound vehicle was impacted by the North bound vehicle on its driver side front door. The North bound vehicle's passenger side collided with the West bound vehicle. There were skid marks made by the North bound vehicle beginning at about twenty feet before entering the intersection, veering West and continuing to the point of impact with the West bound vehicle. The estimated rate of speed for the vehicle was 50 miles per hour, twice the posted speed limit. There were two fatalities in the accident. The driver of the West bound vehicle, a young woman, was pronounced dead at the scene. The driver of the North bound vehicle, a young woman, was found non-responsive and died while in route to the hospital. A baby girl, just a few weeks old, was rescued unharmed from the rear seat of the West bound vehicle. The North bound vehicle was a small black Toyota truck. It sustained damages to the right front and passenger side only, the most severe of which was at the front end and the door. Blue paint from the West bound vehicle was on the door, which folded into the cab of the truck about eight inches. Two beer cans, one empty and the other half-empty, were collected from the truck and dusted for fingerprints. They did not match those of the driver. There was blood on the lower half of the steering wheel which was gathered and processed for DNA identification. It did not match that of the driver. The steering wheel was dusted for prints. Two sets were found, one for the driver and another for an unknown person. The investigator also noted the driver seat was set to the farthest back position. There were three blood drops found in the middle of the seat, on the driver's skirt and on the floor beneath the steering wheel. The drops matched the blood found on the steering wheel. Both doors, inside and out were dusted for fingerprints. The driver's prints were on the handles of both doors, inside and out. A second set of prints, matching those that were found on the beer cans and steering wheel, were also taken from the driver side passenger door. Shards of glass discolored with blood were collected from the passenger side of the truck on the floor and seat. The blood was identified as that of the woman in the truck. Upon impact with the other vehicle, her head had slammed up against the window and her forward shifting body met with the door as it was pushed inward, breaking her ribs, which punctured her lungs. The investigator had concluded that there had to be another person driving the truck based on the evidence collected. DNA and fingerprints found for the unknown person had been sent to the state's DNA criminal database but it did not find a match. He had interviewed the dead woman's family and friends to identify who may have been in the truck with her that morning. He found nothing that led him to a suspect. One of her friends told him that she had recently started seeing someone special, someone who the friend never met or ever heard a name mentioned.

The DA closed the file, buzzed her secretary and told her to contact the police department to see if Al Olson still worked for the department. "If he does, please schedule a meeting with him as soon as possible. If no, let's see if we can track him down." The secretary researched his whereabouts and learned that Olson was no longer an investigator for the department. He had retired after nearly 30 years and gained employment as a senior private investigator with a local firm specializing in criminal investigations for defense attorneys. He was the firm's chief investigator who managed four other investigators. She called the firm and requested to speak with him. She was told that he was out of the office participating as an expert witness in a trial. He would not be available until the trial was over. She left him a voice mail regarding the case that the DA was reviewing and requested a meeting to discuss it with her.

"Mr. Olson, thank you so much for coming in," said the DA. Getting up from her seat behind the desk, she reached out to shake his hand, and motioned for him to have a seat in one of the two chairs in front of her desk as she sat down in the other one. Mr. Olson, sitting down said, "I was so glad to get a call from your office on this case. It was the first case of my career over 25 years ago. I have never forgotten...finding that baby in the car, and knowing that there had to be another person driving that truck. I hope you have something that I didn't." She smiled and said, "Yes, I think I do: a DNA match and fingerprints. We are pretty sure that we know who the actual driver was. Thanks to your detailed investigation and the state's DNA database, I think we can finally solve this cold case. I just wanted to go over the details of the case with you prior to an arrest and filing charges to make sure that we are not missing anything." She learned that Olson had canvassed the neighborhood near the accident and found no credible witnesses. An elderly woman with impaired vision said that she saw what looked like a black guy running off. When pressed for details she contradicted herself multiple times. He also remembered that during the interviews he had a sense that there were witnesses reluctant to get involved.

****

Jake was now employed part-time with Feltonia Community College as a student counselor. His workday was from nine to noon Monday through Friday. He commuted by bike to the campus each morning. He had lost his right to drive years earlier for repeated DUII offenses. Leaving home at eight, he would arrive a quarter after, go to the student restaurant, have a cup of coffee, pastry and smoke a couple of cigarettes before going to his office. One morning, over two years after Lydia Lawson's death, as Jake wheeled his bike through the front gate, he turned around at the sound of a voice saying, "Jake Masters, please come with us." To his left and right were two uniformed police officers. "You are being arrested for the death of Olivia Lawson." Jake shook his head and said, "How many people y'all gonna charge with Lydia's death? Didn't you just arrest some guy a few weeks ago for killing her?" The officer responded, "Olivia Lawson. You are being arrested for the death of Olivia Lawson." Jake grew somber and quiet. "I don't know that woman," he thought to himself. But having been arrested many times, he knew the drill. He raised his hands and said nothing. The officers patted him down, handcuffed him, put him in a patrol car and drove off. He was booked and charged for manslaughter and for leaving the scene of an accident. At the jail, he was interrogated by a police detective working with the DA on the case. Jake did not answer any questions but asked for an attorney. With a public defender present, Jake denied all charges. "I wasn't involved in any hit-and-run accident in 1988 or at any other time. I don't care what you say about fingerprints and DNA, they're not mine."

In court, he chose to dismiss his attorney. He would defend himself. During his three-year stay in prison, he studied criminal law and the rules of procedure every day for about eight hours. He believed that the attorney who was assigned to him in the earlier case sold him out. Despite the judge's admonition, he insisted on a pro se defense. A trial date was set for November 9, 2015. He was granted bail and released later upon posting payment. He was instructed to not leave the state.

In the months leading up to the trial, Jake met with the DA to review the charges and evidence. He could think of no way to destroy the credibility of the evidence so he focused on the investigator. If he could find something wrong with the way the fingerprints and blood was gathered he could try to show that it was not reliable. Despite his efforts, he was not able find what he was looking for. He offered to cop a plea for involuntary manslaughter. The DA rejected it and countered with manslaughter and a minimum of seven years. "The evidence is irrefutable. You were the driver, and you were drunk. If we go to trial, we will ask for the maximum sentence, 15 years."

"I'll see you in court," said Jake. Although he knew the deck was stacked against him, he would take his chances at trial. He had always been good at reading people. Why should it be any different now? He had managed to get his old job back as a university student counselor after serving a prison sentence. He was still working for the college even as he was preparing for trial. He would start with the jury selection, getting the right people in the box. His strategy was to show that he was a victim of a zealous DA out to put another notch in her belt. "Who is she to come against me," he thought with his typical, soaring self-confidence.

At trial, the DA made her closing argument during which she

pointed to two exhibits of photos of Jake: one, of his driver's license, taken in 1987 and the other, of his college student identification in 1989. "If somehow you find yourself questioning the DNA of the defendant or the fingerprints of the defendant, you may want to ask yourself why does the scar above his eye also match the curvature of the steering wheel. Look at his face, before and after. Look at him sitting there, even now the evidence is still written on his face...reminding us of that fateful morning. He chose not to testify, depriving you of an explanation of the scar. Not only of the scar, but he would have had to explain why his blood and fingerprints were there. Don't be fooled, the evidence speaks for him. The blood, a match to the defendant...the fingerprints, a match to the defendant...And the scar, a match to the defendant...Yes, evidence stamped on his face that you cannot ignore. His explanation? He simply denies it all. That's his right...but ladies and gentlemen, you have an obligation to weigh the evidence before you, and to accept the facts as presented. His actions caused the death of two young ladies. He didn't stick around to see if he could help. No, he ran. He gave no thought of attending to a screaming baby girl in the accident, but only of getting away. He ran away and now denies ever having been there. Although he ran, he left behind what only he could leave behind..."

****

Sinclair lay in bed, eyes glued to the ceiling, "Take me, take me, don't stop, give it all to me, aah yes, yes! It's all yours, yours baby, aah, aah, ooowee, ooowee." No matter how hard he tried, he could not drown out her voice or his grunting and moaning in pleasure. He was in jail facing a life-sentence without the possibility of parole. His attorney had told him after reviewing all the State's evidence against him that it was "iron-clad." He said that he could perhaps argue mitigating circumstances or diminished capacity, if Sinclair could show him some convincing facts that would support such a defense. He advised his client that his best defense probably was to cooperate with the prosecution and cop to a plea for the possibility of parole. Sinclair knew that he did not have much to bargain with so he questioned his attorney about what he would have to do to work with the DA. He responded that he could advise on the best strategy for a plea deal only after he heard Sinclair's full story about the facts surrounding the crimes. Why did he do the crimes? How did he gain access to Lydia Lawson's home? Did he plan the crimes? Had he ever been in trouble with the law before? If so, for what? Had he ever been in counseling for mental health? He told him that depending on answers to those and other questions they may be shared with the DA in exchange for a lesser sentence. He went on to say that regardless of how Sinclair answered his questions he would offer (with Sinclair's consent) an admission of guilt in exchange for 15 to 20 years with the possibility of parole.

"Mr. Sinclair, how would you like for me to proceed? To prepare for trial or to see if we can make a deal with the DA?"

"I can't risk being locked up without any hope of ever getting out. I don't want to go to trial."

"Well, let's get started going over the events that led you to Ms. Lawson's apartment. Please tell me about that night."

"Yeah, I wish I had never seen her with him. A tall black man with a scar above his eye would come see her several times a week. At first, before I ever saw him, I would hear them having sex. Lydia's bedroom was next to mine. Since this was happening pretty often and would keep me up or wake me up, I started watching for him. He'd usually come over in the middle of the night (maybe nine or nine-thirty) and leave early in the morning. This particular morning, they were at it again. She was moaning and he was grunting. I couldn't believe it. It was three in the morning. They woke me up! It went on for about 45 minutes to an hour, then he left. After he left, I went over to ask her if she could use her other bedroom to have sex with this guy. I knocked on her door but she did not answer. I noticed that the door was left unlock so I went in and called for her. She was in the shower and heard me. She was upset that I was in her house uninvited and ordered me out. I walked towards her explaining why I was there, and told her that she shouldn't leave her front door unlocked. This made her mad and she threatened to call the police. She went into her bedroom next to the bathroom to get her cell phone. I followed her there and told her not to call the police. She looked at me and said, 'right.' I took the phone from her and she kneed me, just barely missing my balls, and started screaming. I lost it. I just absolutely lost it. The next thing I know, I am looking down at her underneath me, and she is not moving. It was like some kind of bad dream. I don't remember anything until then, just looking down at her and feeling pain in my left forearm. I had some deep scratches just above my wrist, about three or four inches up. You can see the scars are still here. I shook her to try to wake her but she did not move. She was dead. Her face was blue and her eyes fixed wide open looking up at me. My wrists were aching and my arms were burning like I had just finished a real tough workout. I started shaking all over and my head started throbbing."

Stopping briefly to rub his eyes and wincing, "The pain in my head was excruciating. Then I knew it was not a dream. I knew what I had done. I just didn't remember doing it. I still don't. I don't know how this could have happened. I really liked Lydia. I had thought that I could win her over. We could have been more than neighbors." Now cupping his hands together, squeezing them tightly, he blurted out "But I knew when she started seeing this guy that I didn't have a chance." Breathing loud, chest heaving and trembling, he quit talking and said nothing else until his attorney asked him to continue.

"I just could not take one more night of hearing him with her that way. I didn't understand how she could do that to me. I loved her. She just needed more time."

"Tell me what happened after you realized Ms. Lawson was dead. Did you ever check for a pulse?

"No, I knew she was dead just by looking at her. She didn't respond to me shaking her and calling her name. I got up from the bed, put on my pants and t-shirt, went to the bathroom, and vomited in the toilet, washed the blood off of my wrist and wrapped it with a towel. That's when it came to me that I was in over my head."

"Did you put on any underwear before putting your pants on?"

"No, I wasn't wearing any because I sleep naked and I had gotten out of bed in a hurry to go over Lydia's."

Taking notes on his laptop, he nods okay, "Please, go ahead."

"In the bathroom, as I was cleaning up, I realized that I had to make it look like I was never there. I saw a couple of large towels on a shelf. I got them and started wiping down everything that I touched, the mirror, the toilet, the faucets, door knob, the door, door frame and the wall around the door. Everything that I could think of. I went back into the bedroom, wiped down the headboard and the walls around the bed. I could not remember what exactly happened in there, so I wiped down any surface that I could think of, doors, walls, knobs, anything that I could possibly have touched. I went back into the bathroom, turned on the shower using one of my towels. Then I went to the living room, turned off the light, opened the door, quickly cleaned the knobs on both sides of the door. I went back into the bedroom, looked around to see if there was anything that I had missed. I didn't see or think of anything. I rushed out of the apartment and on my way out I turned the living room light back on, locked the door and took the towels with me. "

"What time was it when you left the apartment?"

"I think it was about 5:45AM."

"You said that you looked around the bedroom to see if you missed anything. Any idea how a bus ticket with your prints was there?"

"I did, but I did not see a bus ticket. I use a monthly bus pass usually but earlier that day I forgot it at home. I had to buy a ticket to get to and from work. It must have fallen out of my pocket."

"The DA's evidence says it was found under the bed."

Pushing himself away from the table, the attorney stood up, closed his laptop, and put it in a case. "I have to go now. I have what I need for the moment. I'm going to meet with the DA to see if we can agree on a plea. Once I know what they are agreeable to, I will go over it with you."

Eight days later he returned to Sinclair at the jail. "Mr. Sinclair, I wish I had better news. I met with the DA and they flat out don't want to play ball with us. I was told that the DA is involved in the case, and that she will not accept a plea. They are aiming for the maximum sentence allowed by law, which would mean no parole. They are playing hard ball because the DA made this case a big part of her campaign. I don't think we have anything to lose by going to trial. We could build a defense around diminished capacity to get rid of the murder charge. We could argue for manslaughter, and if successful, you would get parole. Since you cannot remember any details of the rape or of killing her, we would start there. Just so you know, this defense strategy can work only if you subject yourself to psychiatric examinations by a doctor of our choosing and one by the DA. I want you to take a day or so to think about this, then let me know what you would like to do. "

****

"Good evening, welcome to AON News at six. Today in Freewater County Court, Jonath Sinclair was sentenced for the death and rape of Lydia Lawson. Last month AON reported that the court found him guilty of rape and manslaughter. Lawson was a college instructor for FCC and was found dead in her apartment three years ago in March 2013. Sinclair was sentenced to 20 years and will be eligible for parole after 15. This was the second trial for crimes against Lawson. The first trial was against a man identified by Sinclair. The judge dismissed the case when he determined that the wrong man was identified. District Attorney, Jaqui Jones, said that the case was an example of the diligence of her office in prosecuting criminals and getting it right the first time. She was not the DA for the first trial. And in a bizarre coincidence, Jake Masters was convicted in a hit-and-run case from 1988 involving two victims. One of the victims was Olivia Lawson, the mother of Lydia Lawson, who was killed in March of 2013, and whose killer was just sentenced today. DA Jaqui Jones said she is extremely satisfied with the results in both cases and that she fully expects that Masters will get the maximum 'because of his careless disregard for human life, leaving two people to die, as well as a new-born baby; and because of his deception and unmerited freedom all these years.' Sentencing in the Masters case is scheduled for the end of the month. In other news..."

Justin pointed his remote towards the TV, turned it off and left for class.

****